JIM FAIRFAX

CRANTHORPE
MILLNER

First published by Cranthorpe Millner Publishers (2023)

ISBN 978-1-80378-092-4 (Paperback)

www.cranthorpemillner.com

Cranthorpe Millner Publishers

To Sarah

PART ONE

A DEATH

CHAPTER ONE

Death of an innocent man

Stewart Bingham muttered angrily under his breath as he climbed the final few steps and turned the key in the front door of his fisherman's cottage, completely ignoring the sweeping panorama of the picturesque Cornish fishing village below. The view was great, but it was over a hundred steps to get up to the small porch, something he had brushed aside when he made the impulse purchase nearly a decade ago. Now, as time was catching up on him, Stewart was already putting off trips to the convenience store below on a regular basis as his knees kept seizing up. The much beloved tiered front garden had been converted to low-maintenance shingle and a few hardy shrubs last summer by a local gardener. The greenhouse, three panes cracked and the rest mottled with rain damage, stood defiantly on the edge of the flat patio and was verging on an eyesore. So much for his initial plan of a long retirement based around growing his own produce. Stewart made a mental note to attempt to resurrect it in the not-too-distant future. At least the constant dives of the seagulls had stopped recently, seen off by his elderly female neighbour's air rifle.

As he dropped his coat on the sofa and opened a cold beer from the fridge, Stewart was still cursing to himself. Bloody Penny – his agent, Penny Grainger – the whole thing had been her idea. In fact, it was last Sunday when he had been woken far too early, following a late night in the Jolly Fisherman on the quay listening to sea shanties and sinking more pints than he could remember. Blindly reaching for the receiver, she was already talking excitedly, ten to the dozen, at the other end of the line. As he focused on what she was saying, one word stood out.

'Neddy?' he interjected.

'Yes, Stewart. That's why I've rung you up. An appearance on local television. They want to talk to you about the show you did with Neddy. They're doing a slot on retro children's TV programmes.'

Stewart thought carefully. It had been a decade since he'd been axed from the children's TV scheduling, together with his co-star Neddy, a small glove puppet. Since then his career had faltered, with a few years of sparse daytime TV and radio appearances, before he had made the decision to retire altogether from the public eye.

'How much?' After all, he reluctantly admitted to

himself, it may be worth his while for a good fee. Added to this, life had become rather repetitive. He couldn't quite admit to it being boring, but it was definitely repetitive.

And so, he had agreed to Penny arranging today's trip to the South West TV studio in Exeter. They had paid for the rail ticket, although, much to his chagrin, not first class. Stewart was not phased when the taxi pulled up outside the unprepossessing sixties office block on an out-of-city retail park. This was par for the course. No, what had really pissed him off today was the way he had been treated. Actually, no, it was the way he had been ignored. People came and went past him in the small seating area he had been guided to, but none stopped to acknowledge his presence. After being seated with a plastic cup of instant coffee for what seemed an eternity, Stewart checked his watch, and finding nearly an hour had elapsed, approached reception.

'Excuse me, any idea when I will be needed? I've been here an hour now.' He tried to contain his frustration, adding in case they had forgotten, 'Stewart Bingham for the retro children's TV programme interview.'

The shaven-headed young man on the reception desk looked up vacantly from the magazine he had been reading, apparently unaware that he had welcomed Stewart earlier.

'Yeah, no problem. I'll just check.'

He picked up the phone, dialled an extension and nodded for at least a minute as he listened to the reply. Stewart stood by waiting even more impatiently.

'Sorry. They don't need you after all. The guy who used to be in Blue Peter turned up with a new book he's launching. In the end they ran out of time. It happens quite a lot actually. Nothing personal.'

Nothing personal! Noticing Stewart's agitation, he added, 'Still, money for nothing to be fair. You'll still be paid. They always honour that.'

He seemed somewhat taken aback as Stewart raised a single middle finger and then, turning abruptly on his heels, marched out through the entrance doors, calling a taxi as he did so.

The train journey back in a cramped second-class compartment did nothing to improve his mood. The carriage was overflowing with schoolkids for much of the journey and the phone reception was so poor that he could only manage to connect to Penny's number when he was disembarking from the train.

'Never again! A complete bloody waste of time. They didn't even call me. This guy from Blue Peter took up all the interview time. Honestly, Penny, a joke, a bloody joke.'

'Sorry, Stewart. That's bad luck. And I really thought it might generate some work for you.'

He had just been about to reply when the signal cut out again, causing further cursing. And so now Stewart was in his kitchen, a cold beer in one hand and mobile in the other, about to tell Penny not to bother him with any such offers ever again. Full stop.

***

Mid-morning a few weeks later, Stewart was accessing his bank account online when his mobile rang. Seeing it was Penny's number, he ignored it. Bugger it! She could wait after that last episode. He had some limited savings and a small pension, and besides, he had purchased the house outright. He really didn't need the hassle any more. As he checked the account balance, he was stunned by the amount. It was three thousand more than yesterday. Looking through the recent transactions, he saw a deposit from an unknown account for that amount.

The mobile was ringing persistently again and he could see it was Penny once more. Bloody hell, what did she want? Reluctantly, in case she knew of a possible unexpected royalty that had generated the windfall, Stewart picked up the mobile and answered.

'Hi, Penny,' he said brusquely, keeping it decidedly non-committal.

'Stewart, I've been trying to get through to you. Great news. I have lined you up for another interview.' Her voice was breathlessly enthusiastic.

'Hang on, Penny, I thought I told you before, I've

decided to give all that a rest.'

'Hear me out, Stewart.' For once, Penny was beginning to sound impatient. 'This is the real deal. National evening news! They will pay you big money and are sending a car to pick you up. And you are the only interviewee.'

'Really?' Slowly, he was beginning to understand where the money in his account had come from.

'Well, just you and the guy from the computer game company. That's why they want to interview you. The production company has sold the rights for Neddy to be used as a character in a new computer game.'

'Three thousand has just gone into my account, Penny.'

'Wow, they've paid in advance. They must be keen. Apparently, they have used your voicing for the character so there should be a shedload of loyalties once the game is launched. Lucky you, Stewart.'

Lucky me indeed, thought Stewart, as he took down all the details of the interview in two days' time. Door to door in a courtesy limo and the main guest. He went over to the small wall cabinet in the corner of the lounge. He had to admit, it did look like Penny had come up trumps after all. Stewart began to regret the anger he had felt earlier. She had always looked after him with somewhat of a maternal charm even though he was a good ten years older than her. This called for a celebration, he thought. Taking the packet of expensive

Cuban cigars, usually saved for Christmas or his birthday, he carefully unpeeled the wrapping and lit one. Not good for his health, he knew, but what was life if you couldn't treat yourself once in a while?

Moving through to the front of the small cottage, he grabbed his coat and stepped out onto the small front patio. Sitting on the faded bench under the window provided the view of the estuary below, from the narrow harbour entrance with the fishing boats arriving back before the tide left them stranded, to the river snaking its way under the drab grey concrete bridges. Noise rose from in front of the pub close to the Harbour Arm; still closed, it would soon be the first refuge for many fishermen. Yes, thought Stewart, my lucky break has come after all.

***

Several days later, Stewart was seated in the back of an expensive chauffeur-driven saloon as it sped into Central London. The car had arrived in Cornwall early, but cruising on the motorway meant that within three and a half hours, they were close to their destination. As before, he had brought Neddy along in his briefcase, well aware that he would be asked to produce his sidekick at some point. Looking down, Stewart saw the clean white trainers he had dragged out of the back of his wardrobe, matched with some slim-fit black jeans and a hoodie with a trendy hiking firm's logo. It was a long while since he had been on TV and Stewart was conscious that although he had aged relatively well compared to his peers, he was still a man in his fifties. He had seen an article on computer gaming on the news recently; the workers were dressed in casual clothing. He just prayed that he didn't have to descend a curved slide and do the interview from a bean bag!

So it was to his surprise that the reception area of the TV studios seemed unchanged from his time in the business, with the exception of chilled water dispensers replacing the vending machines. No sooner had he stepped out onto the pavement and made his way up the steps than a young woman appeared, smiling at the top of them as she held the doors open.

'Hi, I'm Daisy and I'll be your assistant today. It will be Sangeeta who interviews you, as I said in the email I sent to Penny. Come through and I'll introduce you to the other guest, Mike.'

Stewart followed Daisy through to an area past reception where a large, low grey sofa wrapped around a low coffee table. Perched on the corner of the sofa, a young man in casual clothing was demolishing the array of wraps and sandwiches as if his life depended on it. Stewart sat down opposite, poured a filter coffee and introduced himself. Holding out one hand, whilst still shovelling food in with the other, Mike nodded. After he had finished his current mouthful, he spoke excitedly.

'Great to meet you, Mr Bingham. Have you brought Neddy?'

'Call me Stewart, and yes.' Stewart opened his briefcase and held up the glove puppet.

'Wow.' Mike was transfixed. 'Hey, can you put him on?'

For the first time in several years, Stewart placed the glove on his hand and immediately the puppet came to life. At this point, he became conscious of a small audience that had assembled behind him on the main corridor.

'Look at all these people. What shall we do, Neddy?' Stewart said, acknowledging the interest he had generated.

'Launch the lifeboats, Stewart. Launch the lifeboats!' He said the once-famous panicky catchphrase in Neddy's nasal whine to hoots of delight from the increasingly large group of onlookers.

'Well, it looks like we're just about ready to start filming.' A smart woman in her thirties wearing a casual business suit arrived at the other side of the sofa. 'I'm Sangeeta, pleased to meet you, Stewart. Just to explain, Mike is here as the animator from the company GrooveBunny.'

Stewart raised his eyebrows at this point.

'Who are producing the computer game.' She continued, shaking his hand, she walked over to a door with "Studio 2" written in metallic letters on the front and a large LED sign with the words "recording in progress" flashing above it.

'So, this is where we will be recording. I'll see you back here after you have been in make-up.'

Stewart was not sure why he needed make-up, but he was there for nearly half an hour, while various lights were projected from different angles and make-up applied to reduce the glare off his forehead and cover the broken veins on his cheeks. Some time was spent on the end of his nose – an area that he had noticed had become more red and bulbous recently. He made a mental note to ease off the whisky late in the evening in future. Soon, he was jarred out of his thoughts by Sangeeta, even more radiant after make-up, informing him that the recording was about to start. Talking as they walked, she explained they would be recording now to then broadcast on the early evening national news.

'That will give us about an hour to pre-record a five-minute slot. Don't worry, I'll take you both through each stage of the interview, and then we record these and join them together for the final piece. But then, you would be familiar with all that from your days on live children's TV, Stewart!'

She turned to him, flashing a set of perfect white teeth, instantly making Stewart wish he had taken up the offer of teeth whitening at the local dentist. He had dismissed it at the time as somewhat unseemly for a man of his age.

Sangeeta was a natural at interviewing and the recording seemed to fly by, with Stewart feeling more and more at ease. After the initial introductions, Mike spent some time outlining the process used to create the computer game. The technicalities seemed to be within the grasp of Sangeeta, who nodded approvingly and interjected with the occasional relevant question. Mike explained that they had made a cartoon version of Neddy – referred to as an avatar in the industry – and had generated a voice by sampling from old footage of actual programme episodes. Then she turned to Stewart and briefly outlined his career CV, before focussing on his ten-year stint working on Neddy and Me.

'I suppose at the time, it was seen as an update on The Basil Brush Show?' Sangeeta posed.

'Oh no.' Stewart made a reverential bow. 'No, we could never hope to take on Basil Brush. That was a consummate show. No, from the start ours was intended to be a much simpler affair. Neddy was deliberately made as a simple glove puppet, almost fashioned from a sock. We wanted kids to make their own Neddy. And they did. We had the "Show us your Neddy" slot every week. Kids loved to send in photos of their own creations. And the production team felt it allowed us to generate a strong grassroots following.'

'Well, it certainly did,' Sangeeta agreed. 'At its height, the show had over ten million viewers!'

'Yes, we were always very proud of that,' Stewart continued. 'And of course, each summer we appeared on the network's roadshows, taking Neddy around the country.'

'Perhaps now is the time to introduce him to a new set of viewers and allow some of the original fans to reminisce?' Sangeeta suggested, prompting Stewart, as they had arranged, to introduce the puppet into the interview.

'Hello, everybody.' Stewart produced the glove puppet and put on Neddy's nasal voice.

'Fantastic!' Both Mike and Sangeeta applauded in unison.

'So, tell us about Neddy and Me, Stewart. It appeared impromptu, but was there really a script?' Sangeeta asked, with Mike nodding in the background.

'Well, I hate to break the magic, but yes. It might have seemed chaotic and all off the cuff, but in fact I had a script to learn, including both my lines and those for Neddy. Remember, it was just Neddy and myself unless we had a rare guest, so I had to generate the conversation between the two of us. It really needed a script for that,' he replied.

'Yes, I can see that,' said Sangeeta. 'Did you get many of your own ideas in?'

'Well, not really.' Stewart was beginning to feel somewhat defensive. 'But I did get some of the viewers' mail,' he added.

'Really, are you sure?' Mike seemed surprised.

'Yes, although the vast majority of the requests that we read out were sent into the studio, I did get some sent directly to our fan club address. I read these out, so I suppose that was my creative input. You have to remember that at that time, there was a pretty active fan club.' He hastened to add, 'For Neddy and myself of course. It was run by some of our fans. I just had to pick up the post and reply to the letters every so often.'

'Letters – emails as well?' Sangeeta inquired.

'A few, but we are talking about the early noughties,' Stewart replied. 'Personal emails were not that common back then. And few kids had mobile phones, so no text messages. So it was mainly letters and postcards. It was kids who used to send in the postcards.'

'What was that catchphrase that Neddy had?' Sangeeta asked.

'Launch the lifeboats,' Stewart duly replied on cue.

'We've used that in the game,' Mike interjected. 'We sampled Stewart's voice from the recordings and produced the catchphrase. Neddy is not the main character, so we only needed a few phrases for the different situations he finds himself in.'

***

Once the recording had finished, Stewart shook hands with Mike and Sangeeta. Checking his watch, he was surprised to see that it was already mid-afternoon and he had been in the studio for several hours. As he nodded to Mike, who bounded off with a cheery wave, Stewart checked at reception. Yes, the car would be coming around to the front to pick him up in a few minutes. Then he realised he must have left the briefcase in the studio. Retracing his steps, he was glad to see the door open and the room empty. The briefcase was lying in the corner, behind Mike's chair. Funny, Stewart couldn't even remember walking over to that area. It must have been moved by whoever tidied the room up after the session had finished. Reunited with Neddy, he marched back to the entrance foyer.

It was a typical London day, grey and overcast, as Stewart stepped out through the automatic doors and descended the steep steps to the wide pavement below. Before he reached the car, its driver using the hazards to park on the double yellow lines, his attention was drawn to a hooded figure approaching silently to his left on a large electric scooter. Turning, he moved to take the pen proffered and sign his autograph in the scrappy notebook. No words, not even a whisper, but he was secretly glad to be recognised once more, taking him back to the show's heyday. At that moment, Stewart felt the searing pain just below his armpit. Aghast, he saw the knife still stuck in his side before there was any sign of blood. The culprit was now disappearing into the distance as the limo driver rushed to his aid. Falling, he heard the shouts and screams as the entrance doors opened for a second time. Losing his grip, he dropped the briefcase holding his beloved Neddy. When his head hit the pavement, Stewart was already dead.

CHAPTER TWO

Suspicious behaviour

The old pewter bell attached to the door rang as the next customer entered the shop area. Bunty Regis looked up from behind the cluttered counter, but her husband Bryan had already appeared from their living quarters next door and was now gliding his way noiselessly towards the main entrance. She wished Bryan would give people a little space; he was already strategically placing himself in front of the display of expensive local wines, for God's sake. No wonder customers never browsed for long – it was all so obvious. However, the two elderly ladies who lived in the Edwardian villa overlooking the village green seemed more than happy with Bryan's attention. He was already taking them through the latest expensive additions to the cheese counter, produced by the local farmer.

'Yes, this one is a Kentish Brie, similar to a Somerset Brie but obviously made locally. Oh and that one is local cheddar and cranberry. Yes, of course, you can have a taste of both before you make your decision.' Bryan raised his eyebrows over the bent backs of two customers at a giggling Bunty as he handed them both a few wafer-thin slices.

'Delicious!' they both gushed, as a mixture of cracker and cheese crumbs fell on the carpet.

Ten minutes later, they left, armed with a small basket of rather overpriced cheeses, and a smug Bryan disappeared back into the living accommodation to put the kettle on. The general store they owned served the local community in the small East Kent village of St Margaret's at Cliffe. Adjoining the market square, it was a stone's throw from the well-appointed Norman church, where today the flag was fluttering in the coastal breeze. It all looked rather idyllic really. They were part of the furniture now, of course, having arrived over twenty years ago after purchasing the small shop as a going concern. At the time, Bryan had pointed out that the post office facility would allow them to integrate quickly into the community. Now, they were firm fixtures and arranged many local events throughout the year. Currently, it was the charity jumble sale in the church hall to raise funds for replacing the church bells, one of which Bryan rang most Sundays.

The period after lunch was often quiet with few customers. Bryan generally used the time to attempt the daily sudoku in the lounge, so Bunty was glad of the appearance of Rev Alleyn, who was a welcome breath of fresh air. Her infectious Nigerian laugh and sunny disposition always made Bunty smile. Their main topic of conversation was the possibility of a new Pathfinders club to encourage more of the local kids to come into the church. It was perhaps understandable then that Bunty had not focussed on the late mail delivery and pick-up. She hadn't recognised the postman, but they changed all the time these days.

When the vicar had left, Bunty picked up the small pile of post. Immediately discarding two as bills, she opened the third. Scanning the small note, she was taken back to her previous life, which had been put on hold for a few years now. It seemed Dima was planning something new. This was not a regular postal delivery at all, but a specific drop-off for her eyes only. She placed the slip of paper into her apron pocket as Bryan entered the shop whistling cheerfully and holding two cups of coffee. Dear sweet Bryan, completely oblivious to it all. Thinking on her feet, she spoke first.

'Don't forget I'm off to see Rhona later this afternoon.'

'Really, I don't remember you mentioning it?' Bryan seemed somewhat dejected. A frozen ping meal beckoned, rather than one of Bunty's wonderful homemade creations.

'Oh yes, I mentioned it last week,' said Bunty, more confident of the lie now. 'I did say, Bryan. I haven't seen her in ages and you know how I love to catch-up with her. I think I'll leave in about half an hour to miss the traffic. There's some meals in the freezer. I shouldn't be too late back. If you're not here, I'll check the pub,' she added playfully, jabbing Bryan's expanding beer belly.

'Oh yes, that's true. I hadn't thought of that. In fact, now you come to mention it, I think Jack may need a hand with setting up the quiz night later,' Bryan said enthusiastically, feeling better about the arrangement already.

Later, as Bunty's car disappeared down the quiet country lane, he stopped waving and returned to the cottage through the rear garden, entering via the stable door to the cosy kitchen. He tutted to himself as he surveyed the debris left by the whirlwind five minutes she had spent in there before she had rushed off. Finally, having loaded the dishwasher and cleaned the work surfaces, Bryan picked up the apron that had been draped across the kitchen table. He almost missed the small piece of paper that fluttered down onto the stone slab floor. Squinting quizzically through his glasses, Bryan read the meaningless sentence.

Out of Bryan's view, a few hundred yards away, Bunty pulled over into the empty layby with its little-used footpath to the lighthouse. She opened the glove compartment and took out her small handbag. Looking around to ensure she was not being watched, Bunty opened it and checked she had the sharp double-edged, six-inch knife and her trusty revolver, fully loaded. She had not used either weapon for several years. Intending to catch the fast train from the nearby mainline station, her only concern now was whether she would get to the destination given in time.

***

Jesse Campbell looked out through the dirty caravan window, smeared with grease and dirt. At the farthest end of a somewhat waterlogged farmer's field that had been converted to a rudimentary campsite, its remote location suited him perfectly. He cleared away his breakfast things. There was little in the fridge and he quickly washed the mug and bowl in the sink, leaving them to dry on the drainer. Checking the mirror through the open bathroom door, he hardly recognised himself. Shoulder-length hair and a thick full beard; he knew this was the easiest way to avoid identification. He had been growing it for the past few weeks, ready to shave off as soon as required to create a new identity.

The intermittent drizzle had finally ceased and he had managed to check nobody was hanging around outside the few occupied caravans. Grabbing his bike helmet and zipping up his black leathers, Jessie was locking the door and started his 750cc touring motorcycle within a minute. As his nearest neighbour started to open his window to call over, Jesse was off with a friendly wave, keeping all contact to a minimum. His shift started early in the afternoon and finished just before midnight. It had been pretty straightforward to land the job. His references stood up and he had been able to use the caravan as a registered address. An interview and a few checks later, he was employed as a security guard at the Palace of Westminster, based at the entrance to the House of Commons. From the campsite on the outskirts of a small Essex village, it was a direct half-hour ride down the A13 into Central London, with the added perk of parking on-site.

His instructions had been quite simple: bed down in the job as unobtrusively as possible and wait for further contact via the usual methods. To that end, he had already had two nights out with his fellow colleagues. Both involved heavy drinking sessions with the inevitable bonding over a pissed karaoke rendition or a scrape with bystanders outside the close-knit group. He felt slightly sorry for the quieter colleagues who were, as usual, dragged along enthusiastically by the ringleaders, although in his case it had served the purpose of integrating into the working group perfectly. Now a few months into the job, he had managed to rotate his postings so that he had full knowledge of all the entrances and exits to the buildings.

'Hi, Jesse, are you okay on the front pedestrian access gate?' his boss Shaz called over as he dismounted the Honda. In her twenties, easy-going and remarkably uncomplicated, Shaz had turned out to be a pleasure to work for.

'Sure, no problem.' He smiled back.

He headed through the archway in the grade two listed facade and made his way to the staff room at the back of the building. He had a locker there containing those parts of his uniform that would not fit under the leathers, which he now unpeeled and stashed away. As he did so, Jesse caught sight of locker number B10 on the bottom row, one from the end. By observing it over the past few weeks, he had managed to work out that this was a vacant locker, not assigned to any staff, but was still locked. It was too good to be true. Yesterday he had taken a detour to Amersham to purchase an identical padlock from an anonymous superstore – in cash, of course. Checking the coast was clear, he removed the small hand-held grinder from his jacket pocket and attacked the crossbar of the lock. He managed to get halfway through the inside when he heard footsteps.

'All right, mate! Hangover?' Ed, an ex-squaddie who already appeared to have taken a dislike to Jesse, entered the room.

'No.' He stared up innocently, blocking the locker with his body. Ed was staring at his hair, which was approaching the allowed limit for security staff, with obvious disdain. What was left of Ed's own had been shaved off with a razor. Deciding not to raise the issue,

Ed continued in a slightly more conciliatory tone.

'Well get yer arse in gear then, mate. You're taking over from me and I need to piss off pronto. Comprendez?'

Jesse nodded and made his way around to the small office by the gate. He would have to finish off the lock later.

An hour later and on his coffee break, Jesse was once more attacking the stubborn metal catch. It still refused to yield and he was at the point of giving up when he gave it one last whack with a nearby metal chair leg. Removing the broken lock, he replaced it with the newly purchased near-identical one, which he had purposefully buffed to give a slightly worn impression. Standing back, he was convinced the locker looked the same as before.

Returning to the security office, he nodded to his colleague Gary, indicating he was back, when his phone vibrated inside his jacket pocket. Quickly, he fished out a pay-as-you-go mobile he had been sent about a month ago to replace the previous ageing model. Having read the one message, he made his way directly to find Shaz.

'Hey, Shaz. Sorry, a problem has come up with my elderly gran – I really need to go. Can I leave now?'

'Yeah, no problem. I'll cover for you,' she replied.

'Great, thanks! I should be no more than an hour.' Jesse calculated the return journey from the location he had been sent.

***

'Just these please.'

The young woman handed over some assorted dog snacks and a small, brightly coloured rubber ball. Hardly going to get rich on this, Shona thought to herself, as she processed the contactless card payment and then watched the woman and the small boy leave the shop. He had pointed at the Syrian hamster in a cage behind the counter, but had been swiftly dragged out onto the pavement to avoid a further purchase. Nowadays, Shona made more from home deliveries. Thank God the old Renault had crawled through another MOT. She checked the list in front of her. Four deliveries at lunchtime and she could only afford to close for an hour at the most. It would be tight, but they were all within a few miles and she should be able to make it.

Half an hour later and the faithful Clio was crawling along the edge of a steep hill as it left the pretty Chiltern village of Ibstone. Craning her head upwards to see above the hedge that closely bordered the narrow lane, Shona searched for the top of the white Cobstone Windmill, her final drop destination. The sky was a brilliant blue against the lush green foliage, perfectly framing the iconic building when it finally came into view. The fact that the metal five-bar gate was padlocked did not surprise her. The instructions with the package had made it clear nobody would be at home. Following them, she found the open deposit box that had been built into the gatepost. Placing the small parcel inside it, she slammed the door shut, hearing the mechanism lock as she did so.

Back in the car, Shona hurtled along the windy lanes and back to the suburban setting of the shop in Stokenchurch. Five minutes later, having located a precious parking space, she was turning the sign to "open" and taking up her place behind the counter, having delivered the three large bags of feed and a parcel whose contents were completely unknown to her. Texting just the word "done" to the untraceable number, Shona removed the case and battery from the cheap pay-as-you-go phone and dropped the remaining parts into the non-recycling bin under the desk. They would be collected tomorrow by the bin men before she opened up and would be taken to an anonymous landfill site more than twenty miles away.

Sneaking into the back of the shop for a quick cigarette, Shona kept one eye on the main entrance. Her mind turned to Dima, as it always did when she performed these errands. Ten years ago, he had entered her life. They had enjoyed nearly a year together, before he had explained the need to make a quick exit. If anyone asked, she was to say nothing. She had never known him. That was the plan. Any meetings were purely by chance. Even now, when their meetings were both fleeting and infrequent, he still stirred something in her that none had before or since. He had spoken to her only a week ago, saying they would be meeting up again very soon. It seemed too good to be true. Shona pinched herself and returned to the reality of pet supplies.

***

Dom Stephens moved to the far side of the senior common room and opened the small side window. Smoking was strictly prohibited on-site, but he felt he needed one after the rubbish he had just read through. The university had suggested a Russian module as a subsidiary to its modern foreign language courses. His double first in French and Russian from Oxford had meant the head of faculty, a woman who terrified him with her unflinching demand for robust accountability, had approached him with the request to run the course. At the time, his protestations that the content was likely to be beyond many of the current undergraduates' capabilities was waved away with the abrupt comment: 'I am sure you can make this work, Dom!' Now, several weeks into the first term of lectures, Dom had collected in the first assignment for marking. His suspicions that the content had been above the heads of most students had been well-founded; even the most conscientious had struggled to grasp the basic vocabulary, never mind the constructs and semantics. He had even resorted to taking in simple Russian children's pre-school reading books!

His attention was drawn to a crowd of voices coming down the corridor. Stubbing out the cigarette and flicking it into the flowerbed below, where it joined his butts from the last week, Dom grabbed the papers and made his way over to the pigeonholes, which he thought hardly seemed necessary in this day and age – most missives from above were sent by email with the expected quick turnaround. Most of his superiors were far too impatient to post anything by hand. However, some correspondence still came via the university's own postal service. To his surprise, there was a small white envelope in the slot marked "Stephens, Dominic", alphabetically situated in the middle of the third column. Nodding to a few members of staff he knew by sight, who had just entered the common room, he made his way along the corridor and to his office in the next building.

Jacqui, with whom he shared the long thin space, was away visiting her sick mother. Having listened to the long list of her ongoing ailments over the past month, it was somewhat of a relief to not be greeted by a detailed breakdown of her latest bowel movements. Compared to the rooms of the Oxford dons of Dom's undergraduate days, this box was a depressingly utilitarian affair. Indeed, only the other day he had been struck by its similarity to the end of an aisle in his local DIY superstore. True, it had a window. Some were less lucky. And true, the window looked out onto neither a brick wall nor another window, but one of the few areas of greenery on the site of this once polytechnic, with a small non-flowering shrub as its somewhat symbolic centrepiece. He had plastered the walls with posters from his own French and Russian forays in an attempt to provide a creative environment, rather than just a place to mark essays.

He grabbed the cheap swivel chair and plonked his feet up on the small desk as he opened the envelope. As expected, it was in Russian. Also as expected, it was from Tim Coutts, who he had not spoken to for over a year. Immediately, it brought memories of Dima flooding back. It had been roughly fifteen years ago when their paths had crossed in a Moscow bar frequented by university students. He was on his six-month placement, living with an old couple in a concrete tenement block who were convinced any ailments he developed could be treated with thick cabbage soup. After three nights listening to Kremlin broadcasts with them on their TV and feeling obliged to join the husband playing cards, he grabbed every opportunity to develop a social life more befitting a twenty-something western student. And it was on one of these alcohol-fuelled nights out with a group of like-minded undergraduates that he had been part of a large group entering the popular bar in the lively tourist area just before midnight. Soon afterwards, Dima had joined their group, called over by some mutual friends. Dom was immediately struck by the intense political debate that he launched into soon after introducing himself. He was already recruiting supporters to the cause before the evening was over. At that time, during the free-thinking and outward-looking post-Glasnost era, the appeal was obvious compared to the conservative and protectionist West. It was easy to be swept along with the rightness of it all.

They had become inseparable during the remainder of his time in Russia, as close as lovers, as they discussed home and foreign policy deep into the cold nights. By the time he had left the capital, Dom had become Dima's right-hand man, recruiting others to the cause. Now, he found himself working for a different cause in just as uncertain times.

Inside was a small piece of paper. He read the instructions. Screwing the envelope into a ball, Dom dropped it in the office waste bin and then carefully placed the slip in his inner jacket pocket and returned despondently to the small pile of marking.

Two hours later and armed with a stiff gin and tonic, he was tuned into the amateur radio setup in his small garden shed. Carefully hidden behind a groundsheet in the farthest corner from the door, he had fired it up after closing the blackout blind for privacy from the neighbours. As usual, it took a while to get a clear signal on the correct frequency, but Dom was connected before the agreed transmission time of nine minutes past eight that evening. His call was answered within a minute with the required information. Tomorrow, five o'clock in the afternoon. No location meant the meeting was at the same location as last time.

***

Cheryl Massingham breathed a deep sigh of relief as they trotted out of the Cabinet Office and into the cloisters that ran down to the restaurants and bars. Thank God! Was this what she had fought to be elected for? Middle-aged grey men in suits poured past her, slapping each other's backs in a self-congratulatory manner, gesturing at assignations for a quick drink. Holding her case tightly under one armpit, she made her way to her own office. It was just depressing. All the grand policies that she had hoped would be implemented were moving at a snail's pace, as many of the ministers now raised issues with the more socialist elements of them. And the Prime Minister himself, a man who had fervently campaigned for change, glad-handing and apparently swept up in the complacency of a comfortable first two years, in which nothing had really changed from the previous government.

Arriving at her office, Cheryl was heartened to see her advisor Paul seated at his desk, scowling at the latest missive that had arrived at their door.

'Bloody joke. I mean an utter joke!' His deep Manchurian drawl cut through the still air. He sat back in the chair shaking his curls, looking more like ten than twenty-seven.

'I know.' Cheryl nodded in sympathy. 'Progress is just so slow. I find it unbelievable. Every promised change is more or less blocked on mass by over half the Cabinet, and then a watered-down offering is delivered instead.'

'Old farts?'

'Pretty much. Most of them are in the bar now, congratulating each other on stopping anything of meaning or substance happening.'

'I've booked seats for us tonight at the socialist worker forum over at Brent Town Hall,' Paul announced, a little more brightly, changing the subject. 'Lots of like-minded people. That should recharge your revolutionary batteries!'

'Hardly revolutionary, Paul.' She laughed. 'But, maybe you're right. I probably need some affirmation.'

Ten minutes later, Cheryl left. Checking she was out of the room, Paul sent a text message: "All arranged".

CHAPTER THREE

Meetings

The room in the impressively large architectural masterpiece, which had been a permanent fixture on the square for many years, was sparsely furnished with a small table in the centre and three chairs. The air was warm courtesy of the old soviet-era heating system, which also meant it smelt strongly of stale cabbage, due to the worn lagging. On the two chairs positioned next to each other sat two unnamed officers: one male, one female. Both perhaps mid-thirties, early forties. Dima sat on the chair opposite, staring bleakly back across the table, on which was a coffee percolator, three cups, a small jug of hot milk and a plate containing assorted pastries. So this is the new approach, he thought. Remove the imposing desk. Remove the grand paintings and bookshelves crammed with the nation's great works. Remove the barrier between us and them. Yes, this was the attempt at a new enlightened approach, Dima thought to himself.

Breaking the ice, the man poured himself a coffee and took a pastry, gesturing to Dima to do the same. Whilst he was doing so, the woman, blonde-haired and wearing a smart blue business suit, spoke first. Dima found the pastry reassuringly stale; not everything had changed, he reflected.

'We received news that your recent operation was a success,' she said brightly, as if commenting on a recent music recital. She smiled, displaying extensive dental work.

'Yes, it was a success. It was regrettable, but necessary,' said Dima, smiling back.

'And your agents were involved. Still active?'

'Yes, they are all still operational. Only one was required in the end. It was a simple hit,' Dima confirmed.

'And we understand from your visa application that you will be travelling over there for personal reasons.'

He nodded.

'A relationship?'

He nodded again.

'We have a new operation. From the very highest level. Of course, you have full security clearance, so no problem there.' The man spoke for the first time, leaning forward, rocking slightly on his haunches. His trouser bottoms rose up, displaying taut, muscular legs. 'How are your agents at handling chemical weapons?'

Christ! Dima began to feel the sweat trickle down

the back of his best white business shirt. Thank God he had not removed his suit jacket. Wiping his hand across his face self-consciously, he felt his thick black beard growing back through his skin. He recrossed his legs, took another swig of the now cold coffee and attempted his most relaxed pose.

'Go on,' he replied, as casually as he could muster.

The woman poured herself another coffee and looked on intensely as the man continued.

'We have made contact with a sympathiser of the Motherland. Let us refer to them as Alpha. If they were in a position of control, it would serve our interests and theirs. Your role is to oversee your agents facilitating this. In short, incapacitation of their superiors would allow them to take the role by default.'

'It seems pretty straightforward,' Dima interjected. 'Surely a simple hit. Or poisoning?' he added, remembering some of the most recent state activity.

'If they were close to the leadership, then yes, that would be the case and we would send an agent over to carry it out,' the man replied. 'They are not, although they have a minor role in the current government. Indeed, they are now part of the Cabinet, which is why the opportunity has arisen. Therefore, it will need a major operation; circumstances would then propel them forward to take control. This would allow a large amount of economic and financial support for us.'

'Are you familiar with Novichok?' the woman asked.

'We will be using a derivative developed in our laboratories here. It is soluble in water. This increases the opportunity to spread the effect and makes its transfer easier.'

Dima listened intently as the plan was outlined to him. It was audacious and complex and would need detailed planning for each step of the way. More importantly, each stage would need to be completely unlinked to the next, to reduce the impact of any detection. But it was possible. He could see now why the assassination had been necessary. The integrity of his spy ring had to be maintained at whatever cost.

No sooner had the woman stopped talking than the man looked at his large diver's watch, before standing up abruptly, and nodding towards them both, swiftly issued his apologies.

'I am sorry, I have to leave as I have another meeting to attend.'

As he left the room, the woman also stood up. Dima was surprised to see how tall she was: at least six foot. It now became apparent that it was she who had been in charge of the meeting.

'That was Captain Asimov; I am Major Tanya Kornikova.' As she moved towards him, he could smell her subtle, unexpected scent. Expensive and French perhaps?

'Please let me show you the chemical laboratories.'

Following Tanya down the corridor, Dima was on

more familiar ground. Endless dark, small rooms flanked their path, with the occasional light illuminating a figure hunched over a desk on a laptop, working away on some secret plan or other. This had been his natural habitat for many years. His mind flashed back to the meetings he had had and the deals he had struck behind the security of these doors. Their footsteps echoed on the shiny lino as they strode down the hollow tunnel, encased in the reverberant painted walls. No other sound could be heard – soundproofing still the same as ever. Anything could be happening inside these rooms and nobody would know, Dima thought to himself. All the visual signs he remembered from his visits to such buildings in the past had gone. Great red, black and white posters praising the Motherland and her people, noticeable by their absence. This was a new country now. There was no overt publicity. Instead, it was more subtle than that. This was an economic war, and currency was the king, not weapons.

They turned sharp right into a much darker corridor; just a single low-energy strip light fuzzed away gently above them. Tanya explained this was a shortcut. Less than a minute later, she stopped abruptly, without explanation, and unlocked an unmarked door on the left. Dima noticed it was one of the few rooms without a window in the door. The room was dark and the blinds were closed across the small window. Furniture was piled up in one corner, giving the impression it had long since ceased to be used. A high stack of old folders and papers, presumably ready for shredding, was just visible from the light creeping under the closed door. Destroying the evidence. Evidence of what? As he went to touch the light switch, Tanya placed her hand on his and pushed him against the wall. She placed the key back in the lock, this time from the inside of the room, and turned the key.

Later he mused over how it all happened so quickly. He yielded as she forced herself on him. Resistance, as they say, would have been futile. Hands everywhere and the smell of that perfume again, this time under his nostrils. Their tongues touched and then a wild passion took over.

Later as they dressed separately, she leaned over and spoke in his ear as he was tucking his shirt into his trousers and zipping his fly.

'There is a bond between us now. I will look out for you. Contact me if you need anything.'

Dima nodded solemnly. What was his side of the bargain, he wondered. Suddenly, he felt uncomfortable. He was no longer on such sound footing. A few moments of madness, giving into temptation, had now placed him in a far more vulnerable position than before. His only hope, he consoled himself, was that Tanya had also compromised herself. Unless, of course, this was part of her instructions. Dima wondered whether this was a room she had used for any previous conquests, agreed in advance with her superiors.

Composing themselves, they left the room in small talk conversation, which was in reality unnecessary as the corridor was once more completely deserted in either direction. After what seemed like at least half a mile, with Dima gallantly labouring on despite an aching groin, trying to keep up with Tanya's long strides, they finally came upon a sign stating: "Chemical laboratories". Ahead of them lay further individual signs to a range of laboratories, which Dima assumed must also be accessible via a more conventional entrance. It was clear that the alternative route they had taken was due to the location of the room, where Tanya knew they would not be disturbed.

The freshness of the laboratory hit Dima as much as the bright light that reflected off the white-coated staff. There was no noise. Each person appeared to be fully engaged in their work. Various chemical apparatus were scattered across the desks. Tanya marched over to a small meeting room in the far corner, separated off by floor to ceiling windows. Closing the door behind him, Dima stood while she leant against a new-looking filing cabinet.

'Would you care for a gin and tonic?' she said, revealing those perfect teeth again as she smiled and handed him a glass.

'Well, a little early for me, but...'

'Ice?' she interrupted. 'You would like ice with your

G and T, as you do when you are in England?'

He nodded and she dropped a single ice cube into both their glasses.

'Cheers!' They clinked the glasses.

'Don't drink it!' She pulled his hand away from his mouth. 'You will be dead very soon from a very bad death. The ice cube contains one drop of frozen Novichok.'

'Very clever,' Dima admitted. 'Very clever indeed. Dangerous though, for both of us.'

'It was only in your ice,' she laughed. 'We can't afford to waste this stuff.'

Tanya then outlined how the chemical would have to be transferred as a liquid, but could be frozen to allow it to be hidden, taking effect when it thawed. The question would be how to get it into the UK undetected and then how to pass it on to one of his agents to allow it to be used. There were several routes they had considered, but the one they had chosen seemed the most audacious.

Less than an hour later, Dima was strolling casually towards the far corner of the square, past the crowds of tourists. He wondered how many were actually purchasing postcards and the other tat from the vendors and how many were listening and reporting back to their own agencies. Soon, this will be me, he thought to himself. As he turned the corner and went out of sight, a woman pushing a child in a small buggy paused and sent a text message.

***

'I think…' said Tim Coutts, looking over the top of his large oak desk as he rolled his pen between his thumb and forefinger. 'I think we may have a small problem.' The almost imperceptible lisp was just apparent. His Adam's apple bounced as he spoke, wrestling with the Windsor knot of his fraying silk tie. His high forehead, topped by a few thin wisps of hair, wrinkled slightly as he frowned. The dog at his feet, an elderly beagle, yawned and repositioned itself against the side of the small electric heater that was struggling to heat the draughty room. In front of him cards were carefully laid out from a game of Solitaire, interrupted by Dom's arrival. Tim passed the whisky he had just poured across the table and loosened his club tie.

Dom fiddled with his glasses, taking them off, cleaning them, putting them back on again. He brushed his brown fringe, now flecked with grey, out of his eyes. Inside he was beginning to get that sinking feeling in his stomach. Waiting, for effect, after taking a small gulp of the spirit.

And then, almost casually: 'How so, Tim?' Playing a straight bat.

'Your old buddy, Dima,' said Tim quietly, and almost apologetically.

'Friend. Years ago, yes. Not for a long while now,

Tim. University days, student stuff.' Dom waved his hand as if to quash an unseen unpleasantness. He moved his head slightly to one side. The setting sun had dropped as dusk fell and was beginning to invade his eye line. The room still smelt of the strong French cigarette that had been smouldering in the ashtray since he had arrived ten minutes earlier. After giving the specified codeword, a man in his late twenties had let him inside and then with a nod to Tim, had retreated silently, leaving them to it in the cavernous office. Presumably his latest companion. Somewhere in another room, Mahler was playing quietly in the background. It all felt rather Bohemian, Dom reflected.

'Signs are he may be up to his old tricks again.' Tim leaned forward and eyed him more intensely now, rather like an amateur entomologist with a pinned insect. 'Just a few rumours. We are monitoring it.' And then changing tack, like the boats he loved to sail down in Salcombe at his holiday home. 'How's the family?'

'Good, all good, Tim.' Back on safer ground, but not letting his guard down. 'Kids are both off our hands now, earning money themselves believe it or not. Just the two of us rattling around in that old pile. Still, walking distance to work and the pubs.'

'Yes, indeed.' Tim had clearly had enough of the domestics and moved on to the subject in question. 'So your old pal is returning to our shores imminently. Visa request submitted and successfully processed. Coming over to see a girlfriend. Intending to stay for several months.' He looked down to confirm the name. 'A one Shona McNeil. Ring any bells, Dom?'

'No, never heard of her,' he replied, confidently shaking his head. He had, indeed, never heard of her.

'Runs a pet shop. In a small place just off the M40 in Bucks. We've checked it out and it all seems squeaky clean. The only suspicious thing about it is that it doesn't turn over much money. Not exactly a goldmine. Apparently the two of them go back quite a long way.'

'Really. How do I fit into this exactly? Want me to buy a fish?' A touch of humour.

A long pause. 'Hardly, Dom. No, ideally you would meet Dima by chance. He will welcome you as the long-lost friend you are, Dom. Old chums. We'll run to some meals and a few trips to the theatre on expenses. Then obviously hook up with him and send as much info as you can back to our side. Usual methods, et cetera. Knowing his previous behaviour, it seems impossible to think he will come over to, what is in his mind, enemy soil and not take the opportunity to plan something that could harm our country.'

'And you are sure he never knew I joined your side after my return?' Straight to the point, thought Dom.

'Not at all. Oh no. There was a fall guy, or woman actually in this case. No need for you to concern yourself with that area at all, Dom,' Tim replied. 'Oh no, as far as our Russian friend knows, you still hold those same views. He may well see relighting your fire as a challenge he would relish.' He put the pen down and picked up a cigar from a small wooden box on the desk. As he lit his own, he offered the box to Dom, who declined. Tim leant back further in the leather armchair as he smoked, smiling at the metaphor.

'There is one more thing,' Tim continued. 'It may be nothing, but we intercepted a text message he sent from Russia using an old mobile we had been monitoring. It seems to be a cryptic crossword clue of some kind.' He passed a small sheet of paper across the table to Dom.

Talk about a large bust [9]

Dom shook his head. Nothing came to mind as he studied the words in front of him. As an experienced cryptic crossword solver, he knew it could take time. Forgetting the clue for a moment, he sat forward in his chair, gazing straight into Tim's eyes.

'So this will be an active observation. Something serious afoot?' Don said. He was now giving Tim his full attention. 'How exactly am I meant to do that – suddenly turn up as his long-lost pal after all these years?'

'That, my friend, is what we are working on. Ideally, we need him to be drawn in, to attend an event of mutual interest. When we know, we'll let you know.'

Less than a minute later, the shrill chimes from a large obtrusive cuckoo clock signalled the end of the meeting. As Dom was about to leave, the answer came to him.

'Broadcast, Tim.'

'What?' Tim stared at him.

'The message. "Broadcast" was the answer to the cryptic clue,' Dom replied. '"Talk about" suggests something related to speech and "a large bust", well a bust can be a cast in brass, for example. "Broad" could be a synonym for "large". Quite simple really when you think about it.'

'It's as we thought,' Tim muttered. 'He is coming back and starting something. This is a call to his agents to be ready for his messages. Well thank you for solving that for us so promptly. I have a feeling we will be requiring your crossword knowledge a lot in the not-too-distant future. But our first priority is for you to shadow Dima.'

'I don't suppose I have much choice in the matter,' said Dom, resigning himself, slipping into the abyss. Why couldn't he just solve the clues for them, he thought to himself.

'Well now. We all have a choice, Dom, but we would all be very, very grateful.'

Walking to his car, Dom saw a movement out of the corner of his eye. The young man had returned and was entering the back gate carrying what looked like a takeaway meal.

Later, driving back the twenty miles or so to his own home, Dom racked his brain for common interests he had shared with Dima Kasporov. Of course, there was the politics; that was taken for granted, but that was also too simple an approach. What else had they shared all those years ago? Music – not really. He had already been to see many indie and post-punk bands in the UK, whilst Dima had only shown an interest in the great music of the Motherland. And why not indeed? – Tchaikovsky, Borodin and Rimsky-Korsakov for starters. Not a bad starting line-up, he had to agree. He remembered how Dima hated German composers, particularly Mahler and Bach, although he saved his full venom for Strauss, pop music and Wagner – too patriotic and imperialist. That made him laugh out loud. Had Dima never listened to the full-blown Russian symphonies?

Sport, then? No, as far as he could remember Dima had shown a total lack of interest regarding anything physical. As he pulled up the short driveway, Dom realised this was going to take some thinking. He could, of course, wait for whatever Tim Coutts' bods came up with. But that was what troubled him the most.

***

'Do you think he will play for our side?' the young man said later, in between large mouthfuls of chicken chow mein.

'No problem,' Tim replied confidently. 'He is bored

with that lecturing post. This has whetted his taste buds.' He waved his fork in the air theatrically, laughing at his joke. The beagle was now looking longingly at his plate.

'And he is over the nervous issues in his file?'

'Oh, the breakdown. That was a good few years ago. All in the past,' said Tim firmly.

'Let's hope so,' the young man added.

PART TWO

ONE MONTH LATER

CHAPTER FOUR

Penny investigates

Penny still couldn't believe it – Stewart, dead! Killed in broad daylight on a Central London street. It was just beyond belief. To make things worse, she felt guilty, after all it was she who had persuaded him to take this one last interview, when he made it clear he was content living out his reclusive retirement. And she had asked the police officer a second time, but the woman was adamant. It was a random robbery attempt that had gone horribly wrong. They had carried out a full investigation for the last month. It was the same officer telling her now, DCI Sally Jones, who had delivered Penny the terrible news the day after Stewart's murder. Penny remembered that at the time she had struck her as bright and supportive.

Over a herbal tea seated in the tidy front sitting room, DCI Jones explained that the killer had made their way off on the electric scooter before anyone had been able to apprehend them. Penny remembered how she had read an article in *The Metro* recently, warning of their danger to pedestrians as riders could accelerate faster and reach speeds far in excess of cyclists, mounting pavements and crashing through traffic lights. At the time, having seen relatively few of them, she had dismissed the article as middle-class whinging, although she had also seen an article on the local London TV news, warning they would soon replace mountain bikes as the vehicle of choice for drug dealers in the capital.

Sally explained that as nobody had been able to pursue the killer, the main avenue they had followed had been studying the CCTV from the entrance to the studio and from all the cameras on properties in the vicinity, in the hope of finding a lead. Viewing the footage had taken several days, but the killer had carefully disguised their face within a large black hood, providing no frames that could be used for any clear attempt at identification. The footage from the CCTV showed several employees and delivery drivers entering and leaving the front of the studios. Mike could also be seen descending the front steps about five minutes before Stewart had been attacked. After many hours of painstaking checking, it was clear that there was no evidence of any unaccounted-for visitors.

Sally explained that the actual attack had taken under a minute, with the scooter arriving quickly as Stewart was halfway down the steps. In a way, Penny was glad she was spared from viewing Stewart's last moments, which she was told had been quick, but particularly gruesome. Following the attack, the killer had then jumped on the scooter and shot off into the distance. Electric scooters required no number plate registration and the identification markings had been carefully sprayed the same colour black as the scooter. As it had disappeared from any further CCTV footage, it was more than likely that the scooter and hoodie had been disposed of in one of the large refuse bins that stood outside the back of most hotels and restaurants in this area of the capital. They could even have been dumped in the Regents Canal, which buttressed one of the nearby side streets. Besides, Sally said that the chances were the scooter had been hired from either a shop or a roadside rental outlet. Whichever way, it was unlikely that the killer would have used their own identification for this. Most criminals keep a selection of cloned credit cards and burner phones for this process. And so, after a month of inquiries, leading to nowhere, the police had reluctantly accepted it was most likely a bungled robbery.

'But his watch, his phone, his money, none of these were taken. They were both expensive models,' Penny questioned.

'No,' Sally replied. 'That's true, but it is certainly not uncommon. Very often, if the attacker is disturbed, they make off without being able to take anything.'

'What about his briefcase?' Penny persisted. 'He

dropped that. Surely, they would have taken that at least. He dropped it, didn't he?' she repeated.

'Yes, he did,' Sally replied. 'We did look at that. But we decided that it was unlikely the assailant had time to grab it. They would have had to bend down to the floor. It is likely that they did not intend to stab Stewart, just threaten him, and panicked when they realised they had done so.'

'Was the attack linked to his TV appearance?' Penny inquired.

'No, we don't think there is any link,' Sally replied. 'How can they be linked in any way? Stewart was attacked after the recording took place, but before the programme had been broadcast, meaning that his attacker would not have heard the content anyway.'

'Oh, I see what you mean. And I suppose the broadcast was just a standard interview?' Penny reflected.

In answer to Penny's question, DCI Jones confirmed that they had listened to the radio broadcast, but there had been nothing unusual in the content and it had generated no leads. Penny had also managed to download the interview itself, which was on the radio website as a podcast, and had listened to it numerous times. She had to agree there seemed nothing untoward about it – just a standard interview between a presenter and two guests.

'At the moment, we have been informed by the

solicitors who hold Stewart's will that you are the main beneficiary. He was an only child and both his parents passed away several years ago. They have carried out searches, but nobody has come forward as a relative to contest the will,' Sally had informed her.

Penny was a little taken aback. She knew Stewart was a loner, but he had never mentioned leaving her anything at all. Indeed, he had never even discussed a will or any of his personal finances. Shaking her head as she closed the front door of her smart Hackney terrace on the officer, Penny still wasn't convinced. She knew that Stewart had an expensive watch, a designer one she thought, and one of the latest smartphones, which he always seemed to have clutched in his hand. In fact, now she thought about it, the last time they had met in person he had used it to check his share portfolio.

He had laughed her protestations off by stating it was a necessary evil of retirement. 'Got to keep checking on where the money is coming from!' had been his reply.

Surely either the watch or the phone would have been stolen as he signed the autograph? And then there was the briefcase. He always carried it to their meetings. It was good quality, brown leather and could easily have been grabbed. Besides, for all the thief knew, this could have contained a tablet PC or a wallet. No, the more Penny thought about it, the less sense the police decision made.

Not that she could think at all at the moment.

Builders had descended with gusto on the neighbours' house. Recently purchased by a young couple who never seemed to have set foot in the premises after their initial viewing, it appeared that the whole of the interior was now being refurbished. The cacophony of electric saws and sanders was interspersed with loud blasts from a rock radio station. Her partner was away on a lecture tour in the US. With no kids to consider, it didn't take long to convince herself that a break was in order. Cornwall suddenly appealed. Besides, Penny knew that if she was to get to the bottom of Stewart's murder, she would need to start at his remote cottage.

***

Before she left London, Penny knew she needed to fully check everything relating to the attack. She was familiar with the studios as she had several clients who had either worked or been interviewed there. A short five-minute walk from the underground station and soon she was staring grimly at the scene of the attack. Everything looked the same as it always had done when she had visited in the past. There were ten broad steps – Penny counted them carefully – from the pavement to the automatic entrance doors. She had arranged an interview with Sangeeta and Daisy, who were the only station staff who had spoken to Stewart on the day.

Inside, Penny waited after checking in at reception

and was soon joined by both Sangeeta and Daisy, who arrived together and made it very clear from the start that they had told the police all they knew.

'But we are happy to meet you as his professional colleague,' Sangeeta stated sympathetically.

'And if there is anything we can do to make this horrible experience easier for you, we are more than happy to help,' Daisy added.

After about half an hour in a small side office, Penny had been taken through all Stewart's movements and interactions since his arrival.

'It's exactly as we told the police,' Sangeeta concluded. 'I really don't think there is anything new we can add. The only people Stewart met were the two of us and Mike.'

'How did the idea for the interview come about in the first place?' Penny asked.

'Interesting. We were contacted by GrooveBunny, who said they were creating this game and mentioned we may want to interview themselves and Stewart about it,' Daisy answered. 'I checked it with the studio bosses and the task was allocated to Sangeeta to carry out the interview. We phoned back and let Mike know and then contacted you regarding Stewart's appearance.'

'Yes,' Sangeeta added, laughing. 'I am just a very small cog. I just interview who I am told to.'

Thanking them, Penny walked back to the Tube and tried the number she had been given for Mike's company by the police.

***

As the address was in the North London suburbs, Penny had decided to drive over to speak to Mike at GrooveBunny's headquarters. It seemed more direct than either the Tube or bus and allowed her to stop off at a minimarket to grab a prawn cocktail sandwich and bottle of carbonated water. Now standing outside an imposing Victorian semi with only on-street parking, consuming the last of the crusts, she was checking the address again. Was this really the location for a business? It looked like any other residential street in the capital. Feeling somewhat hesitant, she walked up the short tiled path to the porch. As she looked at the windows, she saw all had the curtains drawn, even though it was daytime. Beside the stained-glass door were two doorbells; one was unnamed. Penny pressed the other, which was labelled "M. Spenta", assuming the M stood for Mike. Still, it seemed very strange that this was a business address. There was the thud of dance music coming from inside the property and she couldn't hear any evidence of the bell ringing at all. Penny was about to walk back to the pavement when the door opened very slightly.

‘Mike from GrooveBunny animations?’ Penny said above the noise. ‘I’m Penny Grainger, we spoke on the phone earlier?’

‘Oh yes, Penny, of course. Come in.’ The door was opened slightly wider by a scruffy Mike, who stepped back into the dimly lit interior. ‘Pleased to meet you. Come through.’

Short and a little portly, he turned and walked down the hall and through a door at the end, darting into a side room to turn off the music on the way. To Penny it seemed like he was wearing some kind of pyjamas as she followed him into a much brighter and surprisingly modern kitchen. She noticed the dragging of one foot, very slightly – a sports injury, Penny wondered. The smell of freshly brewed coffee filled the air. Mike gestured for her to sit down opposite him as he grabbed another cup.

‘You’re just in time. My daily ritual – I grind the beans freshly each day. It gets the creative juices flowing,’ he said, passing the coffee over. ‘Yes, a really sad business. I did speak to the police. I am not sure how much more I can give you. So you were his media agent. You must have known about the interview?’

‘Yes.’ Penny clasped her hands together. ‘And the thing is, Mike, I feel just awful. He didn’t even want to do the interview; it was me who persuaded him. “One last big payday” was how I pitched it.’

‘Well, of course the computer game was generating a

lot of interest,' Mike explained. 'I am sure Stewart would have been contacted for more interviews anyway once it had been launched. It wouldn't have been just the one.'

'Had been? You speak as if the project was in the past?'

'Yes, sadly Stewart's death has meant the company has decided to remove Neddy as a character for the game. It has cost me too. I am freelance. That's how the industry works these days. I am sure you know that as a media agent. Developing Neddy was what I was paid for. GrooveBunny productions is just me, I am afraid. I have other jobs, but this one has dried up.' He shrugged his shoulders. 'You've just got to take it on the chin and get on with the next job. It's a pity though as I really felt it had potential to be a big seller, especially with the revival of retro computer games.'

'Well I am sorry to hear that. Was there anything that struck you as strange about the interview or the day in general?'

'I have asked myself that, but I have to say no. I arrived and left before Stewart, and I only met Sangeeta and Daisy the whole time I was there. The interview seemed to go well. I was leaving with Stewart when he realised he had mislaid his briefcase and returned for it, otherwise I would have left the building with him. Oh my God!' Mike stared at Penny for a second. 'I would have been with him at the time of the attack, wouldn't

I?'

A few minutes later, with Mike's business card securely lodged in her leather purse, Penny made her thanks and left. As the door closed, she turned her head for a last look. Was that really how some tech companies operated, she wondered – just a single person with no real premises? She supposed it was all done online now. After all, surely all you needed was a laptop, wasn't it? Or maybe just a phone. Penny made a mental note to check with one of the tech staff back at the agency.

***

'Pretty much,' was the reply from Darren, the most approachable of the rather aloof small tech team back at the agency offices. 'I've never heard of GrooveBunny though. Not that it means anything. Loads of these companies start and fold every day. I'll ask around for you and post on the technical bulletin boards I use.'

Back at her desk, Penny checked through her emails. One from her boss reminded her that she needed to take her holiday allocation before the end of the month if she didn't want to lose it. Reading through the rest of the message, she was alarmed to see she still had ten days to be taken. She was starting to think she had been working too much – her friends always told her so, and now this confirmed it.

Slowly, a plan began to formulate in her head. Checking through her client list, it was clear to Penny that none of them had any pressing business she needed to work on. Most were up to date with their latest proofs and those promoting new books already had the dates arranged for a good month or so. A quick look at the calendar confirmed that there were no associated events for her to attend within the next fortnight. She knew that Murray Shah, her best friend at the agency, would cover for her if needed. There was always a shed load of admin that was allocated by the partners to the agents like herself, but she would be able to pick this up after she returned and they could always contact her by email if they were really that desperate.

Checking her phone, she rang the number from her recent calls list.

'DCI Sally Jones.'

'Hi, Sally. Sorry to bother you. I just wondered if you had the name of Stewart's solicitors? I thought I'd give them a ring regarding the will, now you have informed me I am the main beneficiary.' Penny tried to sound more confident that she actually felt.

'Hi, Penny. Sure, no problem. They are Trevelyan and Son based in Looe.' She read out the number.

Penny rang off. Checking her watch, it was still mid-afternoon. Hopefully there should be somebody on reception. As it turned out, the call was answered by young Mr Trevelyan himself, or Mr Trevelyan Junior as he introduced himself, although Penny thought he sounded past retirement.

'Ah yes, Ms Grainger. We hoped you might call. We have carried out extensive inquiries and we are convinced that there are no next of kin or distant relatives to speak of who would be in a position to contest the will.'

'It is all a bit of a shock really. I have known Stewart in a professional capacity for over two decades, but we were never that close,' Penny replied.

'Well, I am happy to outline the will for you over the phone. In essence, he left a thousand pounds to the local cat sanctuary – he had a cat, you know, although it sadly passed away last year.'

'No, I didn't know he had a cat. He never mentioned it.' Penny felt guilty acknowledging how little she really knew about Stewart.

'Yes, it was his only constant companion down here, I believe. He also bequeathed a trust to run an annual bursary to support young people starting out in TV and radio presenting. I remember him saying at the time that it was often overlooked or filed under journalism, which he was at pains to stress was not the same thing,' Trevelyan continued.

'Now *that* I can believe,' said Penny, smiling. 'He often moaned to me about how presenters were overlooked as professionals.' And then, suddenly feeling a wave of guilt, she said, 'Oh, doesn't that sound an awful way to talk about him, in the past tense. But he really could be that belligerent. I am sorry.'

'Don't be,' said Trevelyan. 'I am sure he would agree. From my little contact with him, I knew he spoke his mind. Anyway, after that, his entire estate has been left to you as the sole beneficiary. I have to say, he had limited savings and his pension probably won't pay up as you are not his partner, but the cottage is paid for outright and it really is a lovely property. It would make a great home or a holiday let, if you don't decide to sell it.'

'I was thinking,' said Penny, talking slowly as she mulled it over, 'of coming down to look at the property. Could I collect the keys to have a look around the cottage?'

'I don't see why not. Technically, it is not yours yet, but we have already made an inventory of all contents of any worth,' he replied.

'Great, I'll see if I can get down tomorrow. One last thing: any advice on where to stay?'

There was a noise as if Trevelyan was sucking in his breath, once again giving the impression of an elderly man at the end of the line.

'Well, the Jolly Fisherman has rooms, but it may be booked up and it can be a little noisy at chucking out time. It's a favourite watering hole for the locals, but you can't blame them for letting off steam after four days or so at sea. There are also lots of Airbnbs, but again they are often fully booked at this time of the year. To be honest, you could probably stay in the cottage if you have a sleeping bag. It has two bedrooms and I understand the guest room has a bed made up in it.'

'Great, I'll do that,' said Penny, hanging up.

Ten minutes later, Penny had contacted her boss and arranged to take the week of holiday time still due to her, starting the next day. The only remaining issue to be resolved was the transport. Returning to her car to drive home, she gave it a quick appraisal. It was over ten years old and needed a couple of new tyres. It was fine for a short journey, but Penny decided that a drive of nearly five hours may be pushing it. She had visions of constantly checking the temperature and oil gauges. Instead, she checked and saw that there was a direct train from Paddington to Liskeard the next day. She could then change and get the local train to Looe. If she left London at ten o'clock, Penny calculated she should be in the small fishing port at three in the afternoon, leaving plenty of time to pick up the keys before Trevelyan and Son closed. She began packing as lightly as possible.

As she did so, Penny continued to think about something that had struck her as strange during her meeting at the studios. When she had mentioned that the deposit in advance for the interview had persuaded Stewart to attend, Daisy had interrupted her. She was adamant: the company never paid guests in advance, not even expenses. So who had paid the money into Stewart's account in advance? She picked up the phone and called DCI Jones.

CHAPTER FIVE

Making plans

As he did most days, Dom checked his pigeonhole that afternoon only to find an unexpected item: this month's copy of *The Railway Modeller* magazine. He was just about to move it into his neighbour's slot when he decided to give it a quick flick through. His suspicions were confirmed. It was halfway through that he saw a large marker-pen circle highlighting an advert reading "South Bucks Model Railway Club – annual railway layout exhibition and show". The date was in a week's time. So this was the first attempt at a meeting – Dima must have been identified as a model railway fan by one of Tim's contacts. Dom had a sinking feeling. He would have to embark on a crash course to become an expert and even then, there was no guarantee that Dima would even take the bait and turn up. In other words, a lot of work could be wasted. Surely it was more likely he would attend the Boat Show surrounded by wealth and power, rather than a somewhat geeky hobbyist venue. Unless, of course, Dima had another reason for attending.

Dom realised he would have to wait for the briefing details from Tim for any further information that may shed light on this. For now, he would have to familiarise himself with the world of model railways. Reaching into his jacket, he retrieved a small piece of chewing gum – his most recent nicotine substitute. A recent check-up at the university medical centre had convinced him to try and stop the habit he had retained from his student days, albeit on a fairly casual basis. Until recently, that is, when he had begun to find himself turning to the fags more regularly, to relieve the daily monotony of the job.

Leaving the senior common room, he cursed under his breath as he nearly bumped into Gerry Brownlee, an ageing part-time computer science lecturer, who was usually given a wide berth by the rest of the staff. With clothes normally splattered with some of the contents of his last meal and smelling decidedly fausty, he was a walking no-go zone. It was when Dom was at the end of the corridor and heading for his office that he stopped mid-stride. What had Gerry been holding in his clammy paw; hadn't it been a copy of the very same publication he himself was holding? Springing into action and clutching his own copy, Dom bounded back towards the staff room.

Over at the farthest point of the room from the door,

in the small kitchenette area, Gerry was intently pouring the contents of a boiled kettle into a small pot noodle container. Even from this distance, Dom could smell the almost overpowering aroma of pickled onions as the steam filled the air. The rest of the room was now deserted. When he did look up, Gerry eyed Dom suspiciously as he approached him, anticipating the usual form of complaint, only to then let out a small exclamation of joy when he saw the magazine.

'A fellow modeller, well I never. You kept that quiet!' Gerry spoke with genuine surprise. It was the most animated Dom could remember seeing him. A loner, he normally sat away from the rest of the staff, shunning any company. He picked up his own copy, laying it next to him on the work surface, and waved enthusiastically at Dom. 'It's a good one this month. I've just finished reading this excellent article about the restoration project taken on by the Herts and Beds Modelling Society. A team of three, they worked for a couple of years on it. Absolutely amazing,' he continued, opening the magazine to the specific page.

'Just starting out actually. I really wanted some advice,' Dom replied, attempting to change the subject.

It was as if the floodgates had opened. Making his way over to a small cluster of seats, whilst attempting to avoid dowsing his magazine with the contents of his pot noodle, Gerry outlined the different gauges. Apparently, these changed between countries and yes, many people purchased foreign engines and rolling stock. Russian? Well, that was a new one to him, Gerry had to admit, but he would have a look to see what he could find out. He received the latest trade magazines each month and had years of back copies. He was happy to consult these on Dom's behalf. As he chatted animatedly, Gerry slurped his way through his snack, much of which ended up down his threadbare pullover.

'I have a layout showing the Swiss and Italian border. Mountain railways are my thing,' he continued, rather grandly. 'Little engines climbing steep tracks using rack and pinion. Fascinating. And of course, the scenery allows me to create an even more realistic model. Last year, I went on the railway myself. Up the Jungfrau to the top of Europe. Absolutely breathtaking! We were all modellers on that trip,' he reminisced. 'Some partners as well,' he added, in a tone suggesting that whilst this arrangement was not ideal, it had to be tolerated. 'But it was mainly single men like myself, of a certain age,' he confided.

A further ten minutes later, when Gerry had to reluctantly leave to run a student information technology workshop, they had agreed that Dom would visit Gerry to see his layout that evening. It seemed that Gerry had a blank diary most nights and Dom knew he would only be able to convince Dima that their meeting was a coincidence if he had at least some interest in the world of model railways.

***

Worryingly, it transpired that Gerry lived only a few roads away from Dom's own home, meaning that no sooner had he exited his own front gate, than he was beginning to regret his attempts at cultivating a shared interest. This was just too close. The last thing he wanted was to generate a lasting friendship. His interests were much more mainstream – watching sport and socialising with his partner and a group of friends he had known since his teens. Not a reclusive hobby, shared by a few like-minded enthusiasts who, if Gerry was to go by, apparently had no other social life.

He could hardly have missed Gerry's address with the overflowing bins, an old mattress and several broken bikes that littered the front garden. To say it stood out like a sore thumb in the otherwise beautifully preserved row of large Victorian terraced houses was an understatement. It was on a side road that Dom had only used on the rare occasion he had returned on foot after drinking at a local pub situated a further hundred yards away. Following Gerry's instructions, he went around the side of the house and found the scruffy, paint-flaked front door to the ground floor flat. It opened stiffly, under the pressure of Dom rapping the purple door knocker, which was moulded in cast iron to form the shape of a large stationmaster's whistle.

His first impression was that of an old underground wartime tunnel, rather like those Churchill had occupied in a documentary he had recently viewed. The main source of light appeared to be from the small illuminated, intricately detailed trackside models that were dotted around the substantial railway layout, which ran from the entrance into the main lounge area and then through the rest of the flat. It was long and thin, in complete contrast to the oval layouts Dom had owned as a child. Under the sparse lighting, he could just make out the discarded cans of empty energy drinks and overturned tubs of consumed noodles that littered each of the rooms. No, this is not for me, he thought to himself. Just as he was about to quickly retreat out of the front door, there was a loud grunt from a few yards away, followed by the loud sound of someone breaking wind, and Gerry appeared armed with two cans, one of which he held out to within Dom's reach.

'Now let's begin with the engines!' The face that looked at him was almost demonic with pleasure. Clearly, this was a rare opportunity for Gerry to show off his life's passion and he fully intended to make the most of it.

And so began possibly the longest two hours Dom could remember, as he listened to Gerry explaining his layout in full detail. After one sip of the highly sugary beverage, he managed to stealthily leave the can behind the nearest obstruction – a logging plant that sat between the mountainside and the railway line on part of the layout just within arm's reach. Apparently, the track covered over one hundred feet and at several places three tracks were running parallel to each other. The mountains had been hand built by Gerry and then covered with modelling grass dusted by snow, animals, fences, trees and buildings. Dom had to admit it was impressive, and he could see how anyone with a slightly reclusive personality could lose themselves working on such a model. But it was not for him. He was off to the pub at the end of the street for a strong pint. But not before he had secured his final trump card and the reason he had arranged the meeting in the first place.

'Will you be going to the model show mentioned in this magazine?' He held up his copy he had brought with him.

'Where's that? Which one? The South Bucks show?'

Dom made to look in the magazine to check. Of course, he knew it was this show. He had already studied the location for access. 'Oh, yes. That's it,' he confirmed.

'Never miss it.'

'Great. Mind if I tag along?' Dom said. 'You know, to get some more experience?' he added.

'Well…' Gerry pursed his lips. Clearly, he met up with like-minded hobbyists at such events and he was obviously weighing up whether Dom would cramp his style, so to speak. Bloody cheek, thought Dom. Had it really come to this?

'Yeah, go on. Why not.' Gerry nodded, seemingly happy with the decision he had made. 'Welcome aboard, buddy.' He gestured to Dom, who rather reluctantly returned a high five.

Dom left a few minutes later. As he approached the pub, he rolled up the magazine and secreted it in the inside pocket of his jacket; there was no way he was going to be seen carrying it by anyone he knew. Whistling casually to himself, he entered and ordered a pint of real ale, reflecting that he had secured an unsuspecting wing man for his planned assignation.

***

'Excellent. Really excellent. And you say he has no idea whatsoever? That will be great cover for you, Dom. Yes, we have picked up that your old pal is intending to visit the show with his girlfriend. We shadowed him and found he purchased tickets at the local shop in her town.'

'My contact, Gerry, is getting tickets for both of us. I have had a whistle-stop tour of his own layout so I feel I can talk relatively confidently about all this stuff when I accidentally bump into Dima.' Dom felt pleased with himself. He looked at the bookshelves beyond Tim's head, crammed with hardbacks. The academic titles on the spines befitted his host's position as a don at Oxford, specialising in modern European history and warfare. He looked back at Tim. He has aged, Dom thought to himself. He was well aware that he himself was one of the fortunate few who appeared to possess youthful good looks well into middle age, but still, Tim had aged. He looked stressed and Dom thought he could see a vein on Tim's brow that was more prominent than at their last meeting. Not the first time. Dom wondered how he had ended up being part of it all.

'Great stuff, Dom.' Tim leaned forward, his Adam's apple bouncing animatedly now. 'This calls for a drink. Whisky?' He pulled over the bottle of fifteen-year-old Islay single malt, already close to hand on the desk, probably having already seen action some time earlier that evening.

'Yes, thank you.' Dom cut to the chase. 'I still don't see why we have this interest in Dima. Yes, he is politically active – you say he now works for their secret service – but we have no real evidence that he has been responsible for anything here. I mean, has he even been active in the UK?'

Tim cleared his throat.

'You remember the Devon Sea Life centre bombing?'

'Vaguely.' Dom nodded, somewhat reluctantly. He racked his brain and seemed to remember a bomb explosion that was mentioned on the news several years ago.

‘Well, why should you? It was before you started to work with us. No need for you to have given it a second thought. Anyway, he was in the country then. Staying with the same girlfriend. When we delved into the victims, we found something very interesting. Very interesting indeed.’

‘Go on.’ Dom leaned forward.

‘The old man, the children’s grandfather. He had a new identity, called Leonard Gant. Given to him by our sister service. Special Branch were all over it, but Counter Surveillance kept it out of the papers. That would have been fatal. Imagine the publicity. Anyway, his real name was Leonard Kritchev. That is Colonel Leonard Kritchev, late of their service.’

‘A hit?’

‘Looks that way. His wife and daughter and the two grandchildren. And the poor zookeeper that got in the way of course. Collateral,’ Tim added, shaking his head.

‘Just a coincidence?’ said Dom weakly.

Tim raised an eyebrow. He took a short swig of the whisky, leaving the comment hanging in the air for reflection. Picking up the bottle, he offered it to Dom, who declined with a wave of his hand, before topping up his own glass. Once again, he cleared his throat and waited in the silence before replying.

‘As you know, we tend not to believe in coincidences, Dom.’

‘Hard to believe of Dima though. I knew him at the

beginning, Tim. He was committed to his cause, of course, to the Russian ideology, but wiping out a whole family of an ex-agent? I just can't see him doing it. It's too brutal, to be honest.'

'Not just any family. A defector who had been very helpful to us, remember, which was the very worst scenario for them,' Tim added, more seriously now. 'The more I think about it, I think the chance it was a coincidence is very unlikely. True, the explosive was the type used by many terrorist organisations and there was no specific evidence to link it back to our enemy state.' He paused. 'Regarding Dima, you may have to accept it was just a side to him you never saw.'

'But surely there was CCTV? Dima would have been identified. There must have been cameras everywhere?'

'Oh no,' Tim interrupted. 'You misunderstand, Dom. No, Dima was not working as the operative. We believe he was the controller. The spymaster, if you will.'

'So that means…'

'Yes.' Tim finished the sentence as Dom's voice trailed off. 'Dima is the handler. He ran a spy ring here, Dom. We believe he has returned to these shores to take control of it once again, and that means an attack of some kind is imminent.'

CHAPTER SIX

Cornwall awaits

Penny disembarked onto the short platform of Looe station with her sturdy umbrella firmly held high above her head to repel the heaving downpour, which had appeared somewhere between Exeter and crossing the Tamar Bridge into Cornwall. Her memories of the South West were always tinged with some experience involving rain, offset by the pure joy of a dry day spent under the long summer sun. But today, the overcast sky did nothing to suggest any such possible respite, the chocolate and cream paintwork even conspiring to darken the mood. To make it worse, she had left bright sunshine as she boarded the train at Paddington. The rainwater cascaded down the short lane leading from the station to the rows of shops as she followed the few other passengers. There was a sense of inertia in the town, as if it was waiting for the arrival of the first tourists of the season before waking from its annual slumber.

Fortunately, Penny had travelled light, with just a wheeled travel case and light rucksack. Making her way past the local electrical shop, its bargains displayed in the window, and negotiating the growing queue outside the mixed grill takeaway – "full mixed grill for a fiver" – she soon saw a sign for Trevelyan and Son Solicitors, pointing to premises located on the second floor above a hairdressers. Following it to a side entrance and climbing a steep flight of stairs, she was out of the rain and entering a small reception area, standing beside an expensive-looking racing bike. A young girl, barely twenty, was seated behind a cheap flat pack-style desk, partly hidden by a large yucca plant, presumably installed to give a sense of the exotic to the drab little room. Despite Penny's entrance, the girl had not looked up and was still engrossed in her mobile phone, repeatedly saying, 'Getaway!' to somebody apparently called Tracey. On the desk in front of her lay a pile of letters under a pink post-it note with the words "Urgent – please post" in neat handwriting.

'Hi, Penny Grainger, here to collect the cottage keys. I spoke to Mr Trevelyan yesterday,' said Penny, introducing herself. 'Mr Trevelyan Junior,' she added.

The girl looked up blankly from the phone as she became aware of Penny's presence and looked as if she was considering whether to speak, when the door behind her opened and a man in his early fifties entered the cramped area.

‘I’ll take it from here, Brittany, thanks!’

The girl raised her eyebrows sullenly and then returned to her phone.

‘Joseph Trevelyan, pleasure to meet you, Ms Grainger. We spoke on the phone,’ he said, holding out a hand that Penny found had a surprisingly strong grip when she shook it. ‘Please come into the office. I’ll get the keys for you and give you directions.’

As she followed him through, Penny was surprised how young Trevelyan looked compared to his voice when he had answered her call. Indeed, not only was he well-preserved with a thick head of curly black hair, but he was dressed in a sharp business suit and his loose-limbed movement suggested the athletic build of a man who still kept himself fit. Presumably the bike was his, Penny thought. As she looked around the office, the bright yellow Lycra outfit, festooned with garish adverts, draped over a chair in the corner appeared to confirm this. She smiled inwardly as she remembered joking with her friends about the “mamils” they saw each time they took a coffee break in one of the London parks.

Trevelyan caught her looking and laughed. ‘Sadly, I am what they call a middle-aged man in Lycra, much to the amusement of the rest of the office.’ Penny wasn’t sure if she spotted him blushing slightly as he fumbled in a desk draw.

‘Now, here are the keys.’ He handed them over. ‘The

property is Seagull Cottage – you will find out why once you get there! Little buggers are everywhere down here. Bloody pests. Actually, they can get pretty large and aggressive. Some of the locals even take a pot shot at them.' He laughed apologetically, realising perhaps he had overstepped the mark. You have to remember the niceties of some of these city dwellers, he thought to himself. 'I've drawn a sketch map for you, but basically you go back towards the station and cross the main bridge to West Looe.' Trevelyan traced his finger along the map as he spoke. 'Once you are on the other side of the river, turn left and walk along until you reach the fire station. Then turn away from the estuary and head up West Looe Hill. The hill is quite steep and the cottage is about one hundred yards up it on your right.' He drew breath. 'Fantastic views,' he added. 'Mind you, it has been raining. The sea mist can close in and you can't see a bloody thing! It normally clears within the hour. Are you sure I can't give you a lift?'

'I'm fine, thanks.'

He went to hand her his card – an automatic response from a solicitor, Penny thought to herself. She waved it away as she tapped her mobile. 'I've already got your number.'

She left with a final call of, 'Watch out for the seagulls!' ringing in her ears.

The heavy rain had turned to mild drizzle and she had fortunately decided that trainers would be the best footwear for the trip. The pavement was now virtually deserted, although she imagined it was heaving here once the summer season started. Once she reached the fire station, Penny turned up the hill, balancing the rucksack on top of the suitcase, which she wheeled ahead of her. At least the heavy rain had now stopped. It was amazing how so many seasons could occur in one day here. Lost in her thoughts, she almost missed the cottage as it was set back, high on the cliffs. At the side of the road, built into the granite wall, was a silver metal letterbox with "Seagull Cottage (S. Bingham)" written on the front of it in black paint. Beside it was a gate in the wall, beyond which was a steep flight of apparently endless steps disappearing skywards. The winding escarpment was full of hydrangeas and ferns, lush presumably as a result of the warm, wet climate. Penny thought of the dry, sorry-looking plants in her local park, lucky if they got a once-weekly water even in the warmer months. Suddenly, she was conscious of somebody staring over at her.

'S'not been seen for ages.' A young guy, who resembled one of the hipsters Penny often saw in the London bars, loading armfuls of fishing paraphernalia onto the back of a battered white pick-up truck had called over from outside a cottage opposite.

'Yes. Well, sadly, he's passed away,' Penny replied. She immediately regretted being so abrupt – not the best way to win over the locals. In a kinder tone, she added,

‘I am a friend of Stewart’s. It’s all been a big shock.’

‘Ee was no age?’ Scratching his head, the man stooped to pick up what looked like a cluster of lobster pots and buoys.

‘Yes, an accident when he visited London. Very sad.’ Penny stuck to the police story. ‘Surprised you didn’t hear about it on the news?’

‘No, nothing. Not surprised though. London, that’s miles away. You can keep it. And the bloody Londoners that buy up our housing stock!’ He began to sound a little heated.

‘Well, I’m just here to check out his belongings at the cottage.’ Smiling, Penny ended the conversation and turned back to the gate, head down. Pulling her suitcase up each step and with the rucksack now back on her back, she slowly climbed one step at a time. She was glad she had avoided wearing any heels.

Two minutes and several calories lighter, Penny sat down on the small bench by the front door. It felt like a workout at the gym, although that was now a distant memory from well over a year ago. Above the cottage, several seagulls circled somewhat menacingly no more than ten feet above her head. The flat patio area at the top of the steps was small enough to feel crowded by just Penny, the rucksack and the suitcase. Still, the view really was to die for and she could see why Stewart had fallen in love with this location. Now the sun had finally emerged, the unique setting of the town, nestled along the confluence of the East Looe and West Looe rivers, was visible. The cottage itself was in the middle of a terrace of three and had been doused in a clean wash of white paint, as yet relatively unblemished by the elements. Must have been done in the last year, Penny thought to herself. The symmetrical windows either side of the door had empty planters beneath them, ready for this year's planting. Finding the keys, Penny opened the front door and switched on the light. The room looked remarkably clean for somewhere that had last been occupied over a month ago. There was a small amount of post, not the mountain she had expected to find, but then she reminded herself Stewart no longer worked or appeared to have many friends.

Inside, the cottage was small but cosy. The downstairs was surprisingly bright and had been fully modernised fairly recently. It was clear that Stewart enjoyed his home comforts, and the furniture, from the stylish leather armchairs to the solid oak kitchen table, all looked fairly expensive and was in good condition. In truth, Penny felt it had the air of a holiday rental property – a little too sterile for her liking. There was an absence of pictures, plants and general ornaments that can remove the neutral ambience. Certainly no sign of any discarded clutter. A set of shelves beside the front window contained a few detective novels, but was predominantly filled with an array of guides to the local area. It seemed Stewart had purchased every book written about Looe, Fowey and the associated South East Cornwall section of the coastal path.

The centrepiece of the room, however, was a large-scale map of the strip of the south coast from Downderry to St Austell, showing the southwest coastal path, beaches, footpaths and car parks. In full colour, it was approximately three foot by two foot and was suspended on the rough stone wall above the fireplace, which housed a small log-burning stove. This was obviously Stewart's bible and Penny imagined him inspecting it each day before selecting a new route to explore. Looking more closely at the map, she could see the small lines he had made using a fine-tipped red highlighter pen. She stopped counting at fifty lines. These were the walks he had taken. To her, it seemed a solitary life, away from the social buzz of the city. Stewart probably chatted to the people who worked in the beachside kiosks, she thought to herself. With the pubs in the evening, listening to the sea shanties being sung with a pint in his hand and the bustle along the pier when the fishing boats unloaded their catch, maybe he had found a kind of social life here after all.

Penny felt a tear well in her eye; he had been happy here. She bit her lip momentarily. He had been happy here, and she had dragged him away from it to meet an untimely death for a fit, middle-aged man. Of course, she could never have known in advance what would befall him, but maybe she could find the real reason behind his murder. And Penny was convinced it was murder, perhaps because that gave her a little redemption. Perhaps because it made her feel his death was less her fault.

There was nothing downstairs to indicate any interests other than walking. Three pairs of hiking boots, clean and standing to attention, waiting to serve a purpose. One pair, slightly lighter in construction than the other two, were presumably for use in warmer weather. A collection of walking sticks, old rustic and new high-tech, rested casually together against the wall, under a row of pegs holding the latest weatherproof walking jackets. There was no sign of any other sports equipment – no football boots, skis, cricket bats, tennis or squash racquets, unlike the homes of most men Penny had known over the years. He didn't even appear to be a member of the local tennis club; she could just see the deserted concrete courts from the window when she had looked earlier. Clearly, Stewart liked to socialise on his own. But then, wasn't there a local rambling club or walking group? She searched the rooms for any evidence – a flyer on the cork message board, a scribbled note on the calendar that hung from it that might provide further insight into Stewart's life. There was none.

Venturing upstairs, she found both bedrooms perfectly habitable, albeit in the same utilitarian style of most holiday cottage rentals she had experienced over the years. Deciding she would take the spare, Penny laid her sleeping bag on the single bed. Trevelyan had been correct– there would be no need to seek out any accommodation in the town after all. The mattress was reassuringly hard when prodded and felt unused.

Back in the kitchen, she approached the fridge and removed most of the contents into the outside landfill bin. It had clearly begun to smell badly after being neglected for a month. All that was saved were a few stubby bottles of French lager within the sell by date time, which she made a mental note to try that evening. Remembering that she had passed a convenience store on her way up the hill, Penny quickly made a list of provisions she would need for the short stay.

A few minutes later, she was walking back down the lane. It transpired that the shop was part of a nationwide chain and she was soon at the till with everything she needed.

'You're not from round here then?' An immaculately dressed Asian man was standing behind the till, his few remaining strands of jet-black hair plastered down across his shiny brown pate. He addressed her in a broad Cornish accent. She noticed he had not yet touched a single item from her basket.

'No, visiting a friend.'

'You're not buying a house here then?' he said flatly, as he gazed intently at her with beautiful black eyes. 'Or renting one of these timeshares?' he added, as if this was an even worse offence.

‘No. I am checking on a friend’s house. He lives, or lived, up the hill.’ She pointed up towards the cottage. ‘Sadly, he died. In an accident,’ she added quickly.

‘Died in an accident? Who?’ The man changed his demeanour, looking genuinely concerned.

‘Stewart. Stewart Bingham,’ she replied.

‘Oh no! Stewart. Lovely man.’ The man’s kind eyes showed genuine sadness. If possible, they looked even more beautiful. ‘He came in here most days to collect the paper,’ he continued. ‘I thought something was up. He usually takes *The Guardian* each day and *The Observer* on a Sunday. I wondered why he hadn’t collected them. Very sad. I thought he had just gone away. That’s what I told the man who asked for him. Mind you, that was over a month ago.’ He shook his head slowly.

‘Really?’ Penny seized on this small titbit. ‘Someone else asked for him. Over a month ago?’

‘Yes, must have been just before he died. He said he had tried the cottage and there was no reply. I said Stewart was normally around and came in most days. I told him he must have gone away for a bit.’

‘What did he look like?’ Penny enquired, as casually as possible.

‘Well, that was the strange part. Hard for me to tell as he was wearing a motorcycle helmet. I asked him to remove it – company policy for all our stores so we can identify customers.' He pointed to the CCTV camera in the corner of the shop, directed at the counter and the large sign beside it. 'But he just shot off. As soon as I asked, he dropped his purchases and left.'

'Did you see his bike?' Penny asked hopefully.

'Sorry, I was busy serving.'

At that point, a pertinent cough from an exasperated builder behind Penny, holding a sandwich and energy drink, reminded her there was a queue developing. She turned around and smiled winningly at the locals. Paying for the items and with a wave and expression of thanks, she was off back up the hill and up the steps to the cottage.

Later, once she had eaten, taken a shower and changed for bed, Penny got out her laptop and checked the internet connection. She had found Stewart's wifi hub on the kitchen counter by the phone socket, together with the password on a small card attached to the back of its casing. Surprisingly, the signal on the laptop showed a strong connection. Hunched over the kitchen table, she checked her emails and was relieved to see no messages from work, just a lot of junk mail, which she promptly deleted. Putting her own laptop away, Penny saw Stewart's computer lying under a pile of magazines on the table. As expected, it was locked. She tried the most obvious password, "Neddy", but to no avail. Pouring herself a glass of rosé, Penny racked her brains to think of the most likely password. She tried

“Stewart” followed by a variety of numbers, including his age, fifty-two, and digits from his date of birth, 1968. After several failed attempts, a message informed her that the laptop was now locked.

Penny remembered that she had seen a small antique-style bureau upstairs in the main bedroom. Evening had closed in and it was now almost pitch black upstairs. Rather than switching on the lights, she took in the view from the landing window looking out to the channel, the small town laid out below her. The sea and the river estuary glistened, giving it a magical appearance. Switching on the bedroom light, she closed the curtains and moved over to the bureau. It looked like an antique, made from a beautiful walnut veneer. Out of character with the rest of the furniture, she imagined this had been handed down as an heirloom.

The top drawer was clearly where Stewart had kept his most important documents. Here was his chequebook, ISA savings account documents, property deeds, insurance and utility details, and his passport. Penny took each of these out and checked through them. Everything appeared to be exactly as you would expect. DCI Jones had explained that the wallet holding his credit card and photo driving licence had been found at the scene of the attack. There was also the latest copy of his will prepared by Trevelyan. It had been signed and dated within the last year and confirmed what she had already been told about the distribution of his estate.

There were two more drawers. Penny opened the middle one. It was almost empty, except for a collection of photos stored in their developing envelopes that all appeared to be holiday snaps. Most were photographs of picturesque locations, occasionally with small groups of people posing in them. Stewart appeared in a few of the group photos, but there was nothing to suggest anything more than groups of friends enjoying each other's company on holiday. Nothing to suggest any close companion or significant other. Penny noticed some of the more recent photos were of Looe, with a couple of the cottage, the road below and the path up the steps at the front. These were the keepsakes from the life he had started here, she reflected.

Lastly, she opened the bottom drawer. Penny was taken aback by the contents. It was crammed full and as she removed items, more were revealed underneath. Several envelopes and manila folders appeared to be stuffed full of letters and postcards, together with ten VHS video tapes in individual boxes with handwritten labels, each stating a year, from 1997 when the show had started until its last year, 2010. It had been a long time since Penny had seen a video tape; indeed, she had thrown her last video tape player nearly a good decade ago, when everything had switched to DVDs. There was also a pile of photographs, all identical, showing a youthful Stewart holding Neddy and smiling into the camera. Penny thought back to the recording of

Stewart's interview, remembering how he mentioned the fan mail and requests to be read out on the show. Maybe this could shed more light on his murder. It would appear that none of the correspondence had been seen or categorised by the police. Taking a pen and paper and the first folder, Penny worked through the letters first, making a note of anything that seemed unusual.

Three hours later and Penny had a very clear idea of the adulation Stewart had enjoyed in his heyday. Over half the communications were requests for signed photographs of either Stewart, Neddy or both of them, explaining her earlier discovery. The rest appeared to be personal requests to be read out on the show. The majority were birthday requests for children. Penny noted the ages tended to be between six and eleven, clearly the target age range for Neddy and Me. There were also some requests from parents or grandparents. Penny worked through each of them, a laborious task, making notes on anything that seemed out of the ordinary. After an hour, she had refilled her wine glass and lit the log burner. Checking her watch, she was surprised to see it was approaching midnight and was just about to call it a day, when she stopped in her tracks. Something was not right. She read the latest postcard again.

Hope to see you at the party tomorrow! Don't forget your cowboy outfit and gun. Nikolai.

This seemed a little sinister for a request. Was it a party invite? Also, she was sure she had seen that name before. Penny picked up the pile of those requests she had already checked and flicked back through them once more.

Five minutes later, she had found the handwritten letter on pink paper, watermarked with balloons, inside an envelope.

Dear Neddy, please can you say hello to my friends. We are all going to the Sea Life centre in Devon this week for my birthday. I think we will have a blast. Thank you, Nikolai Johnson.

Penny froze. How many boys called Nikolai would write in to the show? This had to be the same person. But that wasn't what worried her. She looked at the date of the franking on the envelope. It confirmed her worst fears. Three days after the letter had been sent, a bomb had killed ten people at the Devon Sea Life centre. She remembered; it had been on the news. At the time she had been shocked that such an attack had taken place in such a remote spot in deepest Devon. A whole family had been wiped out.

***

It was just after three in the morning and Penny couldn't sleep. It didn't help that the curtains did not cover the whole of the window in the spare room, and the roller blind did little to stop the harbour lights and the full moon shining through. But she knew the real reason was her discovery. In effect, this linked Stewart to two attacks: his own and the bombing at the Sea Life centre. While she had been lying awake, another thing had gnawed away in her mind: new suggestions for the password to Stewart's computer. After all, several hours had passed since she was locked out from the failed combinations. Reluctantly, she gave in to the idea of forgoing sleep until another time and descended to the kitchen to make a herbal tea and try to access the laptop once more.

The first two attempts failed and then she remembered the date Stewart got his break on TV with Neddy – 1979. "Neddy97" worked. Checking his emails, she hoped to be able to find more correspondence from fans. She was in luck. Stewart had transferred all the emails relating to the show to a folder entitled "Neddy requests".

Progress in analysing the emails was much faster now Penny knew what to look for, and she found one request straightaway that looked suspicious.

Nik says thank you to all his friends for the necklace.

Could this be Nikolai Johnson, and wasn't a necklace an unlikely present for a young child? Penny made a note of the email address and the message on her iPad and copied the text to a Word document. She had almost given up when she spotted another similar message, sent a year earlier.

Present found in unchecked place. N. Johnson.

So this could be Nikolai Johnson. It may not be. However, the request seemed stranger the more Penny read it out aloud. It didn't seem to make any sense. Was this really a request at all? No, Penny was sure it was not. It was too cryptic. That wasn't to say of course that Stewart hadn't read it out on air anyway. In fact, the more she looked at it, the more it looked like a cryptic crossword clue.

Giving up, Penny switched off the computer and decided that at four thirty, she may just get four or so hours' sleep. Ten minutes later, she was wide awake again. Her literary brain was firing away and the solution to the clue was staring her in the face. "Present found in unchecked place" meant a present found from the letters that made up "unchecked place". She froze as she checked them again in her head. All eight letters were there: NECKLACE.

Suddenly, she remembered the videos. Under Stewart's TV was a video player. Considering how old it was, the lack of dust suggested it had been used on a regular basis, and this was confirmed by the wear on the play and eject buttons. The question now was, did Stewart read all the messages out live on the programme? Fortunately, he had labelled the tapes by year. Checking the dates on the postage and emails, she found the shows for 1999 and 2001, the two years in question. It took a while playing with the remotes to get the first video tape displaying on the TV, and then some further time fiddling with wires to get any sound coming out. Eventually, the screen came to life, reminding Penny of the poor quality of the tapes back then, made even worse by the fact they had been recorded from the TV and had clearly been viewed on several occasions. Each show had a surprisingly short slot, about fifteen minutes, although these were bulked up by commercials – the usual products for children's programmes, namely cereals, sweets, fizzy drinks and the latest toys. She marvelled at how far society had come in just over ten years. Not just the products, but the delivery and the social attitudes all seemed so outdated.

An hour later and she had seen all she needed to. In all the excerpts, Penny watched how Stewart's delivery was identical: relaxed and enthusiastic, with a glimmer of mischief in his eyes. Each of the four messages had been delivered similarly in Neddy's nasal tone and there was nothing to suggest that Stewart had noticed anything amiss when reading each one out.

CHAPTER SEVEN

Recruitment

It was many years earlier when Dom had first been approached, if it could be called an approach, for this line of work. At the time, he was just out of a long-term relationship and at a loose end, when an email appeared in his inbox advertising an event for alumni of his old Oxford college, Corpus Christi. Normally, he would have deleted it without a second thought, but something about the location, the Radcliffe Camera, appealed. His appetite was further whetted when he saw the talk, which looked deathly boring and was to be delivered by a renowned economist, would be followed by a string quartet recital and a five-course meal. It was when he looked at the blurb about the musicians that he made his decision. Dom had carried a torch for Fiona Chang since she had spoken to him in his first week, as they waited to collect their mail at the porter's lodge.

Now he was unattached, and still, in his opinion, reasonably presentable, he wondered if there could be a chance at romance a second time around. His few attempts during their time as undergraduates had been met by pleasant but firm rebuffs, due mainly to her preoccupation with a constant stream of male companions. Maybe now would be his chance at last? A look in the mirror confirmed it may be worth a try. Having just returned from a week in the south of France, courtesy of the university's language department, Dom possessed a bronzed youthful appearance, exuding vitality and vigour. Checking the email, he saw the date was the following Friday, giving him just enough time to get his dinner suit dry-cleaned; last time he checked, it still had some stains from a friend's stag weekend several months ago.

***

Dom felt noticeably less confident when the evening arrived. Having booked himself into a modest hotel, situated within walking distance from Broad Street where the festivities were to be held, he had driven the twenty miles straight after his last lecture, arriving just before six. He had already begun to realise the night was going to be an expensive one once he totted up the fifty pounds for the ticket and the cost of the hotel, and that was before any drinks he managed to buy Fiona.

It was one of those beautiful summer evenings that showed Oxford at its best, and Dom's spirits rose as he strolled from Summertown towards the Martyrs' Memorial and St Giles. He had left early, allowing a detour via the edge of the university parks. As he drew on his second cigarette, he reminisced on the time he had spent lying on the crisp grass in the early summer months during his undergraduate days, still only recently behind him. Whilst students keen to get their university blues had toiled away on the cricket pitch, he had spent much of his time sharing a bottle of wine with like-minded friends. Checking his watch, Dom saw he was still early. He took a walk towards the small wooden pavilion, fresh from a new coating of white paint for the start of the season. He could smell the strong fragrance of the flowers, now in full bloom, that bordered the path. Inevitably, his thoughts turned to the failure of his latest relationship, and with that, thoughts of how different his life may have been if he had dated Fiona Chang. By the time he had entered the Broad, via a quaint alleyway he had remembered from his student days, he was in a heightened sense of expectation.

As it turned out, much to his disappointment, Fiona never appeared – ill, apparently, and replaced by an older woman who had no link to his time at the college. Fed up after a wasted evening, listening to a rather pompous city trader who liked the sound of his own voice, he was about to call it a night when a short stocky man with thick glasses and an ill-fitting dinner suit waved at him from further down the other side of the fifty-foot-long refectory table, as the final course was being cleared away by the waiting staff. Dom recognised Mark Jennings immediately, despite the time that had elapsed since the last time they had spoken on their graduation day. They had both been linguists at the college, although Jennings had read German, rather than French. It had been the Russian tutorials they had shared, as part of a small group of four undergraduates who bonded over the alarming lack of support provided by the elderly don assigned to their tutorials. Usually late, if he deigned to turn up at all, he had spent hours standing with Jennings in the cold corridor outside the locked wooden door. It had been the two of them who had taken it in turns to hammer on the solid wood in the vain hope of a response.

Dom had always found Mark good fun. There was always a sense of mischief in his eyes staring out from behind the strong prescription lenses. Spotting a free seat next to Jennings, Dom slowly negotiated his way over.

'Hey, buddy!' Jennings shook Dom firmly by the shoulders. 'How's things?'

After an hour of bemoaning their current lives and reliving the halcyon times as undergraduates, Jennings suggested they remove themselves to the college bar, where many of the guests were already heading. Although it was now dark, the passageways were well lit as always by lamp posts, showing the university never slept. They passed The Bear public house, with its formidable tie collection making it a popular tourist haunt, and heard the chimes on a college clock sound the hour, almost in defiance of sleep. As they plunged down the spiral stone staircase and entered the small bar, the atmosphere brought Dom's memories flooding back. The crypt-like room was lit by candles placed in the small alcoves that had been cut into the stone walls centuries ago. There was a queue in the far corner, where the small serving area Dom remembered well was struggling to meet the demands of a far larger number of customers than a normal Friday night.

'Find a seat while I get the drinks,' Jennings almost ordered, as Dom wandered off through the throng. Finding a seat was easier said than done and he couldn't really see why they couldn't stand like virtually everybody else. But when Jennings returned holding a small tray with two pints of bitter and two whisky chasers, he was quite insistent and gestured for Dom to grab a table and two chairs, which had just been vacated by an elderly couple.

'There we go,' said Jennings, as he placed the drinks on the small round table. 'That should keep us going for a bit.' The table wobbled violently and Dom wedged a folded beer mat under one of the legs.

'I still don't see why we can't just stand like everybody else? After all, we've been seated all evening.' Dom looked around at the mass of people standing around them as if to make his point.

'Well, careless talk and all that. This is more private,' Jennings replied, taking a sip from his bitter, before downing the whisky in one go.

'Private, really? I can't see we have anything to discuss that's private!' Dom snorted with derision.

'When I explained to you what I had been doing these last few years, there may have been some details I omitted.' Jennings leaned forward, tapping his nose in a knowing fashion. 'You see, I had to be sure,' he concluded, leaning back once he had finished.

'I don't know I follow you? Had to be sure of what exactly?' Dom replied, trying not to appear obtuse. He was sipping the whisky and bitter tentatively now. He could feel the large amount he had already drunk that evening beginning to take effect.

'Oh yes. But I am sure now. Quite sure.' Jennings seemed adamant.

'Sure of what?'

'Sure that you are fed up with your current situation – your job and your social life – and up for a new challenge. You more or less said so yourself earlier.'

Dom stared at him, trying to focus a little more clearly. It was true. He was at a loose end and he liked the idea of some new excitement or challenge. Jennings swiftly changed the subject and nothing more was said on the matter until they parted just before one o'clock. As they shook hands, Jennings slapped him on the back, informing him rather ominously, 'We'll be in touch!'

To be honest, Dom felt rather relieved the evening had ended. After their chat, he had watched Jennings turn slowly into one of those characters who he always tried to avoid: loud, the centre of attention and determined to make an impression on everyone they met. He had drunkenly flirted with a woman in front of her unimpressed partner and then insulted an elderly don, who had nipped in for a drink in a familiar bar that he had presumably previously considered a safe space.

Thirty minutes later, after a perilously drunken walk along Banbury Road, Dom lay snoring like a baby, fully clothed on the hotel's double bed.

***

It was several weeks later, and the incident had slipped to the back of his mind, when Dom received a telephone call to his landline. He reached the phone on the tenth ring, surprised the caller had not hung up.

'Is that Dom Stephens?' Dom wondered who else it could be as this was his landline and he lived alone. He didn't recognise the voice.

'Speaking.' He assumed this was a call relating to work, although he had never been contacted by phone at home before. He braced himself. It was most likely to be some jobsworth from the bursar's office, querying his allowance claim from the recent French department trip. Thinking about it, he realised the claim for the meal in the swanky restaurant on the last evening was rather excessive. At the time, he had wondered whether it would get rejected, so he really only had himself to blame.

'Great! I am an associate of Mark Jennings. I understand you met up with him recently?'

Dom baulked somewhat. He wasn't sure why anyone would know of or be interested in his social life, let alone his meeting with Jennings. And what was an associate? Surely people were either family, friends or work colleagues?

'My name is Tim Coutts. I wondered if you were interested in a little additional work? For the government,' he added.

There was a long pause. Dom hadn't expected this, and he needed to reflect on it. Sensing this, Tim cleared his throat and continued.

'Of course, there will also be suitable remuneration. But make no mistake, this is no ordinary job.' At this point, the man laughed gently. 'And this is not real life.'

***

It was a few days later when Dom was seated opposite Tina Di Scrursk, his head of department. He was already beginning to regret asking for the meeting. She clearly had little interest in what he was saying, but experience had taught him to lay his cards on the table to avoid an explosion at a later date, even if all the cards were deliberately not visible. This was definitely a case in point. In a way, it was good that she was clearly paying little interest to what he was saying. Her dyed blonde bob was almost hidden behind the upright computer screen, as it had been on his arrival a few minutes earlier. Having launched into a whining monologue about the poor quality of his students, he was greeted, as expected, by the occasional dismissive grunt, whilst she ploughed through her mountainous inbox.

'And one last thing.' He inserted it in full flow. 'I have been offered some paid work and I understand from my contract I need to inform you of such.'

Her head appeared fully above the laptop screen, but she was still only half listening and waved a hand in dismissal.

'No problem. Just let Rowena know the details on the way out.'

That was it. Dom rose, summarily dismissed, and made his way to the door. His hand was on the handle when he heard the fateful words.

'What type of work exactly, Dom?'

'Translating. Russian.' He gave his pre-planned response.

'Really? Very interesting, Dom.' She had taken her glasses off and was giving him her undivided attention for the first time. ‘What type of translation exactly?’ Her voice sounded much crisper now, fully focussed.

‘Oh, just some work for a twinning association between a town where my brother lives and one in Russia.’ Surely she wouldn’t need any more information. He had thought the cover story through as far as this point – just enough to explain the appearance of the deposits from the fictitious translation business Tim Coutts had informed him would be the cover for all remunerations for his most appreciated work.

‘Thanks, Dom.’ Her head was back down again. Lost interest as he had hoped. He opened the door and entered the outer office, relaying the information to Rowena, despite the fact that she had no doubt been listening to most of what had passed between them.

***

And so it began. When Dom reflected back on the experience, he realised he had never heard from Jennings since. Tim never mentioned him and he could only assume that his work was separate from his own, despite Jennings’ initial suggestions otherwise. Perhaps his role had been purely recruitment?

CHAPTER EIGHT

Leaving Russia

Dima almost missed his flight. He had only himself to blame. The night before he had finally succumbed to the advances of Tanya and Asimov and met them for a pre-operation drink in a crowded backstreet Moscow bar. As the heavy rock music blasted out from the throbbing speakers, drinkers crowded into the small space, swaying to the pulsing bass lines. He had to shout over the screeching guitar and wailing vocals; to be honest, he felt out of his comfort zone – everybody else looked in their twenties or younger. To make it worse, out of his uniform and in straight jeans and a tight white T-shirt, Asimov struck an even more athletic figure, accentuating Dima's own shambolic appearance. His balding head and mottled skin made him feel suddenly self-conscious compared to the fresh-faced complexions of his two companions; he had already noticed their pristine dental work at their previous meeting. It seemed everyone with money under forty in

Russia now had their teeth done, Dima thought, as his tongue ran over his gaps from missing molars and he became aware once more of his developing overbite. He made a mental note to investigate a quote for similar work himself.

Six rounds of vodka later and an evening of Asimov's bad cop routine meant that Tanya won him over with hardly any effort. As the two of them left together, she informed Dima that she was engaged to Asimov, but that they had a "free" relationship. Her numerous lovers were a necessity due to his startlingly low libido, which contrasted with her high sex drive.

'All he seems to think about is keeping fit,' she moaned, as she held tightly onto Dima's hand. 'And not the type that involves me. Just gym, gym, gym whenever he gets a spare moment.' Her breath smelt strongly of alcohol and the sweet mixers, as he knew his own did. He could feel his world starting to spin and made a conscious effort to focus on the neon lights ahead.

The rain had started, pelting down hard. It was not quite hail, but it hurt his bare head enough for Dima to put on his woollen hat. He was glad now of his nondescript waterproof jacket, holding it protectively over Tanya's exposed shoulders to avoid her getting drenched, while valiantly trying to keep up as her long legs sped across the wet cobbles. Dodging the late-night revellers, they stopped at a Turkish restaurant that was still open, to savour a tired-looking kebab and some strong black coffee. The owner smiled knowingly; this was the time when lovers, young and not so young, had the city's late-night cafes to themselves. Much to his disgust, Dima noticed the man give him a rather smutty wink and made a small grunting noise as they left, fortunately unheard by Tanya.

Back in the tiny bedsit, hidden down a complex rabbit warren of lanes, the noisy heating system clunked through the night, masking much of their loud lovemaking. He guessed this was not the residence of a high-ranking secret service officer, but more likely a convenient location used purely for such purposes. This seemed to be confirmed by the bed sheet that had been hastily draped across the small window, hiding the flaking paint of the frame. A calendar hung unused on the back of the door. No posters or pictures. Indeed, there was little sign of any personalisation on the whitewashed walls, devoid of any individual touches other than a mirror and a crucifix. This was confirmed when he opened the door of the bare wardrobe on the one occasion when she had left the room to prepare them a coffee. It was par for the course. Some things still hadn't changed that much from the old days, he thought to himself.

Gymnastically bouncing into a variety of positions on the ageing metal bed, Dima woke after less than three hours' sleep feeling physically drained. He regretted it immediately afterwards, of course. He knew he had compromised himself yet again. In his mind, Dima mused over the possible implications of his latest foolishness. He had shown weakness and he knew he would be likely to regret it. What other reason could there be for Tanya's interest in him other than some form of honey trap? Dima shook his head sadly. Ten minutes later, while she still lay motionless on the bed, he was out on the cold side street, his breath visible as he walked. Daylight was beginning to take over from the brightly burning sodium-vapour street lights as dawn broke.

On the crowded tram ride back to his penthouse flat on the other side of the city, he breakfasted on fresh oranges from a corner shop and threw back painkillers with warm bottled water. Even at this relatively early hour, the tram was filling up. Despite it being a ride of over twenty minutes to the other side of the city, he stood by the doors, rather than sitting. Looking around, he saw mainly office workers in their neatly pressed clothes, interspersed with the occasional construction worker heading for one of the ever-increasing number of building sites. Fortunately, Dima had already packed the day before, but just before leaving he made a further check of all the hidden items. Still, he had to smile at the ingenious nature of the plan that had been hatched the night before, although he could not take all the credit; Asimov and Tanya had sewn some of the seeds.

The key, as always, was to avoid detection and, failing that, avoid further links that any detection may uncover.

A last-minute dash through the rush-hour traffic to Vnukovo airport from his flat in a taxi followed. Dima was last to check in as the gate was closing, meaning he was lazily bade on his way with a cursory wave from an overweight bored customs official, looking up momentarily from his glossy magazine. His Russian passport showed the standard state-style photo, matching his sombre casual attire. He smiled at the welcoming cabin crew as he boarded and made his way to his seat – the only one that now appeared to be empty. He carefully scanned the cabin for any interested parties. He had not meant to be late, but it did have the added benefit of possibly identifying anybody who may have been waiting for him; that is, anyone who was only travelling on the flight for the sole purpose of shadowing him. There was mild interest from a family seated halfway down the aisle, but he also noticed a head of straggly grey hair rise slightly behind a broadsheet newspaper in the second row. Other than that, his entrance appeared to have gone unnoticed.

The plane was packed in economy, something he relied on to provide greater anonymity, compared to individual, unwanted attention of business class. He took his aisle seat next to a couple who were so heavily petting each other, they didn't even notice his arrival. Dima placed his rucksack between his legs, rather than above him in the cabin locker. He had considered placing the items that would be of most interest to British customs in his case, which was hopefully safely stored in the hold, but decided instead to carry them with him in the rucksack. After all, the present had been safely wrapped in several layers of packaging and the mission would be pointless if it mistakenly disappeared to Copenhagen, Lisbon or somewhere else courtesy of the state airline.

As the plane started to taxi, preparing for take-off, Dima opened a cheap paperback thriller he had purchased a few days earlier to provide a focus for the relatively short flight, and ordered a meal and glass of Hungarian chardonnay to fill the time. He had been dozing for nearly an hour, when the grey-haired woman he had seen staring over her paper when he boarded bumped into his left leg that had splayed into the aisle.

'Hey!' He jumped up in pain.

'Apologies.' She glanced down, opening both hands in a defensive gesture. He noticed they were clad in white leather gloves. The accent was not Russian, perhaps Eastern European, but the pronunciation of the one word told him enough.

The rest of the flight passed without notice, although Dima remained vigilant. There was the usual performance of waiting at the carousel on arrival at Heathrow, with the added sideshow of the more impatient passengers fighting to get to their cases. Of course, Dima's was of no importance. It was the rucksack cradled on his front that carried the precious cargo. However, he knew that taking the case, filled with clothes he would hardly use, presented greater cover when he passed through customs. Dima was beginning to sweat as he made his way along the seemingly endless walkway to passport control. He waited for what seemed like an age as the young female official studied the document.

'Thank you.' She handed the passport back. He nodded and moved on towards the customs area and headed for the large sign bearing the words "Green Zone – NOTHING TO DECLARE".

Dima realised he was sweating even more profusely now as he walked through the entrance to the narrow corridor, undoing a further button on his white polo shirt as he approached the small group of officers. Thankfully, it was not a dark colour. They would pull him over; he knew they would. Slowly, it dawned on him. Had he been poisoned? His mind raced. The hit had been on the plane; it had been the grey-haired woman. His leg was throbbing more intensely now, on the calf just above the ankle – was this where the poison had entered?

'Your case, please.' He placed it on the counter in front of the middle-aged customs official, a large man, squeezed into his uniform, whose disinterested appearance probably belied his investigative powers.

‘And your rucksack,’ a second officer, this time female, added.

All he could do was stand back and wait. The case was checked and handed back within a minute. Then the rucksack. He looked away as they removed the contents, one by one, onto the counter.

‘What’s this?’ said the man, holding the package suspiciously.

‘A birthday present. For my girlfriend’s son.’ He had practised the lie beforehand, of course.

Dima winced as the man shook it, looking at the professional wrapping. Ribbon, tied in a bow. He hoped the small flask didn’t spring a leak, for all their sakes.

‘What is the present?’

‘A model train set.’

The man handed the parcel to the woman. She picked up a pair of scissors and made an incision in the far corner. Peeling back a small amount of the wrapping paper, she held the parcel under the light. Dima imagined she was looking for some evidence to verify the contents. Nodding, she handed it back. In a few seconds, the rucksack and case were handed back.

‘Enjoy your stay.’

Briskly, but trying to avoid breaking into a run, he wheeled the case as casually as possible towards the toilets, some ten yards from the end of the exit of the customs area. As soon as he was in the cubicle, he opened the rucksack and poured the contents of a mineral water bottle down his throat. Noises coming from the cubicle next door – loud vomiting – did nothing to make him feel any better. Then he pulled up the left leg of his trousers and inspected the swollen area. There was no obvious mark other than a small red bruise amongst the dark hairs on his white flesh. Dima thought for a moment. He was pretty sure it was more dangerous to take an antidote pill if there was no poison. In fact, he knew it could be fatal. He made his decision. He would know in a few minutes if he had made the correct one.

***

Leaving the toilets five minutes later, it struck Dima that perhaps he had overreacted. As well as feeling much better, he had almost stopped sweating completely. Surely, an experienced operative like himself was not suffering from nerves? Besides, this was not his first visit to the UK. He managed to locate a trolley and weaved his way through to the arrivals lounge, past the family reunions and stressed-looking business travellers. His heart sank as he saw the redhead in her mid-forties staring intently at the stream of visitors. For once, she had dispensed with her usual scruffy sweater and was wearing a smart crew neck, ironically topped with a necklace of pearls. His smile went on as he strode boldly ahead to continue the relationship he had started several years ago for purely selfish reasons, and that had served him very well, thank you, in the years since.

'Darling! Dima! Over here!' She was waving frantically in his direction, pushing past others to the front of the waiting crowd.

'Shona! Darling!' Pretending to have just seen her, he picked her up in his arms, sweeping her off her feet. As he did so, his mind drifted back to Tanya Kornikova. Different perfume, her scent still under his nose even now.

'It's been so long, more than a year. I just couldn't believe it that you were coming. I have been waiting for you, Dima. All this time, I have been waiting.' She was breathless, giddy-headed with this newly stoked love, dragging him now towards the exit and the car park beyond. He looked around as they walked away from the terminal building. There was no obvious reception party, despite the fact that his visa application meant the secret service would have been informed of his arrival. He was a little on edge as they wound their way up through the throngs of stationary travellers.

Dima had not realised they needed to take the lift to the ground level and the car parks beyond. He kept his eyes fully on the other occupants, a couple of middle-aged men, aware that this would be a perfect location for a hit. One of the men frowned back and then looked away and spoke in hushed tones to his partner, who looked ahead at the door as he listened. Dima craned his hearing to catch the language. Not English. Northern European, maybe German or Dutch. It seemed like an eternity as the lift descended. Once again, he reflected how easy it would be for himself and Shona to be killed in the lift. A brush against them with a shoulder bag, chemical poison lacing the name tag, not yet removed. A tap against the back of the calf, from a poisoned toe cap. A gas canister released by assassins now wearing masks. All these methods were well known to him from the field reports he had read. He felt the sweat running down his back once more.

To Dima's relief, after what seemed like an age, the doors finally opened. He held Shona back with a subtle hand on her arm, ensuring they waited until both men had departed the lift. Never leave your back exposed was the first thing he had been taught all those years ago.

Striding purposefully over to the parking bay, Shona opened the hatchback boot and Dima deposited both the rucksack and case inside.

After three attempts at starting, the old car rattled asthmatically into life and soon the airport buildings were in the rear-view mirror as they were trundling down the slip lane, gathering speed to join the M25 orbital motorway. Dima's smile was fixed. God how she talked, he thought to himself. Non-stop! He nodded every so often in agreement as they followed the signs for the M40W and Oxford. His mind drifted as he remembered what a central location it was when he had first stayed over with her. Close to London. More importantly, close to motorways leading to the rest of the country. As the little car raced along the motorway, a joint conspirator willing them on, Dima looked out at the lush green landscape that flashed past on either side. He remembered the hymn he had heard being sung during his one visit to a church service in England; this certainly was a green and pleasant land.

He thought of the Necklace spy ring and the agents he would be making contact with once again in the near future. His role as a handler was a delicate one. The plan was in place and he needed to ensure all operatives were able to fulfil their roles. In his mind, he had already allocated the different tasks, like parts of a jigsaw. He had already alerted them with a simple text message. As before, Dima often relied on the use of cryptic crossword clues for instructions.

The traffic seemed to be heavy in the opposite direction, but the motorway ahead was clear, and it was only a few more minutes before Shona was parking the car in a bay outside the shop and opening the boot. Clutching both the case and the rucksack, he followed her past the rubbish bins assembled for collection on the pavement, through the front door and up the steps to the flat above the independent business. His nose was immediately attacked by the smells wafting in from the premises below, particularly from the bags of animal feed stored in the backroom and from the rodents' cages. The living area was smaller than he remembered from his last visit, with a sofa and chair clustered around a small tired-looking television set. In its drabness, it closely resembled many of the outdated apartments he had visited back home, in complete contrast to his own high-tech bachelor pad. The strongly scented candles that Shona was hurriedly lighting appeared to do little to improve the ambience of the place.

Looking down through the rear window, he was reminded of the depressing view over a small dirty yard, littered with old sacks and half-opened boxes. Behind it lay a narrow lane providing access to a block of old garages. He could see the uninterrupted country beyond. It all looked very peaceful. Dima pondered over whether to probe Shona later as to their suitability for storage. However, his eyes were drawn to the grey squirrel perched on the locked wooden gate in the high rear wall. It always paid to survey all access points.

Shona looked expectantly at him and he almost missed his cue, but then threw his arms around her, before excusing himself for a shower. Standing under the slow, lukewarm trickle of water, it struck him that he had not brought her a present, not even flowers. A potentially catastrophic oversight on his behalf – any committed lover would have arrived weighed down with presents. Fortunately, he had some sterling in his wallet and a trip to the local shop may just save his blushes. Changing in the bedroom, he placed the rucksack carefully under the bedside chair.

'I just have to nip out to the nearest bank,' he explained, as he entered the lounge again, drying his hair as best he could with one of the threadbare towels he found hanging on the rail in the bathroom. He always liked thick pile luxury himself now he could afford it, and the towel reminded him of poorer times. 'Just have to register my card for use in the UK. I won't be long. Shall we go out to eat when I get back?'

'No need, I've prepared a nice romantic meal.' Shona smiled back. 'There are a couple of banks in the town.'

'Great. I'll get some wine as well while I'm out.' He put his leather loafers back on and swiftly descended the stairs.

The small high street was surprisingly well-served with an array of independent stores, cluttered fashionably along the main thoroughfare. As befitted an upmarket location, most of the shops had only a few browsing customers. Fortunately, Dima managed to purchase some expensive artisan chocolates from a trendy-looking boutique and a suitably large bouquet from a florist. It also gave him a chance to check his mobile. No new messages since the one he had received last month confirming the death of the children's presenter.

***

Back at the flat, he tried his best to generate a suitable response to the romantic atmosphere that greeted his return. In addition to the candlelight, Shona had slipped into a figure-hugging dress with a plunging neckline and had applied a further layer of make-up. She was a very attractive woman.

'You shouldn't have, Dimi,' she cooed, using her pet name for him as he handed the gifts over. 'And this too?' She drew the present out from behind her back and waved it around in front of him, laughing coquettishly as she did so.

Dima stared. His pulse ran quickly. She had been through his rucksack!

'I am sorry, I know I shouldn't have looked. But I was so excited! Can I open it now?' She made to tear the wrapping paper.

He took it off her slowly and then smiled.

'It is a surprise – not yet. I am saving it for the right moment,' he said. 'You understand, of course?' She looked at him in mock dejection.

'Of course, Dimi. How romantic. I'll let you tease me!'

He had to admit, the meal really was delicious, and after three glasses of chilled rosé and a selection of assorted chocolates, the bedroom beckoned. It was not wasted on Dima that less than twelve hours after leaving

Tanya's bed he was now sharing another's.

Afterwards he lay awake staring at the ceiling, while Shona dozed blissfully in a pink satin negligee with one arm draped across his chest. The roots were beginning to show through her dyed hair, Dima reflected, and she had not removed her make-up. Once the persistent soft snoring confirmed she was soundly asleep, he disentangled himself and crept along the corridor to the small bathroom, grabbing his mobile as he left. Seated in the dark on the toilet seat, he sent two photos and a short text – enough information to get the full message across. Then he returned, exhausted, to the bed and slept peacefully through until morning. When he awoke, the bed was empty and he could hear the sound of Shona singing in the shower.

***

Dima realised he had created a new and rather awkward task for himself, but it couldn't be helped. He needed to purchase a gift in a box of the same size; thank God she hadn't opened it. He would have to re-use the wrapping paper, which he purchased from a municipal supermarket back home; it was unlikely he would find anything even vaguely similar on sale in provincial Buckinghamshire and he didn't have the time to go to London. Perhaps it was available in the stores on Oxford Street aimed at an international audience, but after some deliberation, Dima dismissed this as a little over the top. Instead, he convinced himself that Shona was unlikely to notice the small rips if he taped it carefully back together. He hit on the idea of a short trip to Reading. The cover story would be seeing a fellow countryman, a friend who was studying applied physics at the university. There would be no time for him to go shopping as he needed to catch up on vital news. Shona was welcome to join them, of course. As he was single, they would be meeting at the friend's bedsit on the university campus. As Dima suspected, Shona refused the invite, instead choosing to spend the time in the large shopping mall in the city centre. Dismounting at the bus stop in bustling Reading, Dima was reminded to be back there in two hours to take the shuttle back to the park and ride.

Immediately he followed his smartphone to the local jewellers and purchased a reasonably priced nine carat gold necklace – rather ironic in the circumstances, he thought. Sadly, the assistant, whilst very helpful, was unable to provide him with a suitably sized box. Instead, it would have to be a case of switching the items in the boxes.

With a good hour still on his hands, Dima made his way to the large park in the centre of the city. Soon he spotted an unoccupied bench in the farthest corner away from the crowds wandering along the main walkway. Here he carefully took out his burner mobile and checked for messages from his controller. Dima had not met the controller. He had no idea if they were male or female, young or old, or where they were based geographically. There was no need. Contact was infrequent. He would be contacted only when necessary and even then, only in extreme circumstances. Somewhat to his relief, there had been no contact made to the agreed number.

After they had returned in the early evening, Dima managed to change all the items on the pretence of having a bath. The water filling up the bath behind the locked door masked his frantic attempts to remove the wrapping paper whilst retaining at least some of it intact. There was the added problem that the dampness in the air began to make the paper moist, meaning Dima had to perform the whole process in a very short time frame, which he managed to do. And so, after placing the railway model in the slightly smaller box, he was able to present Shona with the box she had held the night before, but this time, on the pretence of an anniversary of their first meeting – she had forgotten, how clever it was of him to remember – and see her delight as she opened it and tried on said necklace.

CHAPTER NINE

Further liaisons

Dom chose to sit down in a faded brown leather club armchair, which, although extensively worn, proved to be surprisingly comfortable. This time, Tim had met him personally at the front door, his arms outstretched – '*Mein host*!' – and led him promptly through to the spacious lounge at the back of the property, with panoramic views overlooking a large green paddock beyond. Tim's cheeks seemed redder than last time and small veins had become visible on his skin's surface. Dom noted there was also a much stronger aroma of dog than on his previous visit. Outside, a horse raised its head lazily over the wooden fence, looking uninterestedly in through the window. The room itself appeared to have been furnished by a job lot purchased from a cheap antique shop; several of the chairs looked worse for wear and the rugs on the floor were faded and more than a little threadbare. In fact, perhaps it had been a junk shop, Dom reflected. Or perhaps they were family heirlooms; some years back, Dom had idly researched Tim's background and found the family was at the very least landed gentry, with even some links to royalty.

Once again, this room, in the same way as the study, was verging on a fully functioning library with dark oak bookcases covering every available part of the walls that was not a door or window. Some of the books looked ancient, their colourful leather spines all faded, but Dom also spotted a large number of paperback editions of modern classics. It looked like the ancient shelves would collapse under the weight of the burgeoning tomes.

Several minutes later and both were now armed with a large glass of chardonnay, Tim uneasily sprawled on an old brown fabric chaise lounge across the low occasional table from him. In fact, it all looked slightly incongruous. At nearly a foot taller than Dom, Tim was all arms and legs, his spindly limbs sprouting from the rotund beer barrel-like body. Dom felt quite neat in comparison. Tim was wearing a pair of loose-fitting mustard cords and a thick white Aran sweater with leather patches on the elbows, despite the heat generated from the blazing radiators. Dom had already felt the need to remove his jacket and loosen a button on his new designer polo shirt. Flicking his fringe out of his eyes once more, he noticed his glasses were beginning to steam up as the temperature in the room appeared to rise.

'Did you enjoy the magazine?' Tim spoke first, soon after they had settled down, the glint in his eye suggesting some amusement.

'I am developing a strong working knowledge.' He smiled thinly. Was Tim enjoying this, he wondered.

'Great.' Tim paused slightly. 'I have a little more information I can share with you regarding our friend. Dima arrived yesterday via Heathrow. He was met by his "girlfriend".' At this point, Tim raised his eyebrows markedly, suggesting what was in his opinion a somewhat dubious arrangement – a means to an end, perhaps. 'He then travelled, together with his deux valises via her small car, to the flat above the aforementioned pet shop on Stokenchurch high street. Customs pulled him over and searched all his baggage thoroughly – they had their best people waiting for him, all arranged in advance from our tip-off – but nothing was found.' At this point Tim stopped, somewhat crestfallen.

'He is far too clever to be caught that easily,' Dom replied. 'I am sure he will get some items through undetected. When I knew him, he prided himself on being a master of covert activities. He will have looked on it as a challenge to get whatever it is into the country undetected.'

'That,' said Tim, leaning back, 'is exactly what we are worried about.' He stared blankly to a point above

Dom's head, apparently in deep thought.

'What surveillance do we have in place?' It seemed a little impertinent, but Dom reasoned he may as well check what safeguards had been arranged. After all, he was going to be the main active counter intelligence agent and therefore the person most at risk. Surely it was only fair that Tim shared the full details.

'Marcus – you may remember him from your last visit?' At this point, Tim casually waved his hand. 'Has taken up a trainee position in the florist shop opposite the girlfriend's flat. Not much fun for the poor guy, but he keeps up surveillance whilst learning how to flower arrange and serve the "gin and jag" set of South Buckinghamshire.' Tim shook his head slightly, clearly missing Marcus, but accepting the move was for the greater good. Dom nodded. It made sense. It also explained the smell; obviously, Marcus had run a slightly tighter domestic ship.

'In fact, Dima has already been in and purchased a large bouquet. Over thirty pounds. Quite the romantic touch. Marcus served him. Said he looked pretty washed out; "drained" is the word Marcus used. He was impressed by his English though. Only the slightest hint of an accent. If you weren't listening for it, you would miss it, he said.'

'Yes, he is an excellent linguist. Part of the reason why he has become so integral to their plans I would imagine,' Dom commented.

‘In addition, we have his mobile phone tapped,’ Tim continued. ‘Of course, he is too savvy to use this for any serious planning. But he may always make that one mistake that leaves the door open and lets us in. For example, leaving it on while he is travelling.’ Tim tutted. ‘I mean, model bloody railways. I ask you! Golf, yes, okay. Sailing, we can all appreciate that. Even squash or tennis. But model railways.’ He snorted with derision. ‘We think there’s something not right there. Still, it would, of course, make an ideal cover for a handover.’

‘How?’ Dom interjected.

‘Well. There will be a lot of items on display, Dom. And I am sure it is not uncommon for some of the visitors to handle them. Certainly, those who claim to be experts,’ Tim continued.

‘Yes, I can see that now,’ Dom said sagely.

Indeed, Dom saw very clearly. His experience of counter intelligence may have been limited to less than ten years, but one of the key aspects he remembered from the covert training was the importance of the handover. Passing information in briefcases via railway platforms, lost luggage or even public waste bins. He remembered the lecture from one of the field agents, who recalled the handover of papers inside the cardboard of the popcorn container, left for him on a vacated cinema seat. This was another ingenious method. Lots of people milling at a convention, passing models to each other to admire. All that was needed was the minimum sleight of hand. The oldest trick. Replace something with something else that looks identical, but isn't. Most of the time it really was that simple. Sleight of hand.

'Where's the location?' Dom asked.

'Ahh, now that's very clever. An old Victorian school building, now used as a village hall and for a small local playgroup. They are just happy for the money of course; it's a cash-strapped venture like most these days. Tiny village, in the Chilterns, near where Dima is staying. Just a Friday to set up and Saturday for the show.' He fired the information rapidly at Dom, like bullets.

'Let me guess. Old building. Occasional usage. No CCTV,' Dom interjected.

'Bang on. Got it in one. Only installed at the pub at the entrance to the village. Nice place – The Cow and Butcher. Popular with the wealthy, not cheap, but always busy. People drive there from miles around, car park stacked with Porsches and Bentleys. Been there myself a few months back actually and felt rather conspicuous parking the Land Rover. It has two cameras mounted on the front of it, one facing each way. Both a good hundred metres away from the venue, which is at the top of a small lane running off the postage stamp-sized village green. Still, they should pick up any visitors to the village, unless they use the side road down from Watlington. You turn up with your new buddy nice and early and keep an eye out for Dima. Ideal cover if he spots you, couldn't believe it was him, et cetera. What are the chances of this? Old friends – a reunion in order after all these years. Your new railway fan buddy will be the perfect innocent foil, a great wing man. He will act totally innocent because he is totally innocent, completely oblivious to the shadow dancing going on around him. In the meantime, most importantly, watch out for the handover.' Tim paused for breath and stared at Dom as if to emphasise the importance of the final point.

Dom had to agree, it seemed like a foolproof plan. He was about to go when he saw in Tim's eyes there was something more. Half out of his seat, instinctively, he sat back down again.

'Of course, we want to know the content of any conversation. Take this,' Tim continued, as he handed over what looked like a new mobile phone. Dom held it in his hand and turned it over. Surely it was just a new mobile phone?

'Switch it on.' Tim gestured. It operated as any other smartphone, all the apps, etcetera.

'Keep this on at all times and use it instead of your own one. It has an extra feature. Once you get to the venue, switch on the weather app. It displays a fake weather page, complete with realistic data, but actually loads a channel that will pick up all speech within ten feet at perfect quality and feed it back to our technical bods. They will be inside a large removal van parked up outside the vicarage in the next village.'

Dom nodded. It was indeed an ingenious little device. He was beginning to realise there was a lot riding on the proposed meeting.

***

Cheryl settled down into her seat on the back row, sipping from a takeaway coffee, a small oat milk americano in a cardboard cup emblazoned with a trendy logo. A deliberate ploy, hidden away from view behind the occupants of the chairs in front of her, namely several belligerent-looking men who appeared well past retirement. She had chosen a navy wool jacket, faded designer jeans and a pair of pink high-fashion trainers to give a trendily casual, dressed-down look, although she realised now that it was rather in contrast to her well coiffured, blonde highlighted hair. She was beginning to worry the outfit may be a little too reminiscent of a "Sloane Ranger", or maybe a newsreader. That would be fatal in this setting, which had all the ambience of a working man's club. Cheryl applied a little more red lipstick. Paul had disappeared to mingle with several influential-looking people, but she was intent on keeping a low profile, just a few nods and handshakes as she had entered the town hall. She could see him now, throwing his head back and laughing loudly. He really was a very attractive young man. Of course, she had turned up out of a sense of duty as the local MP. No doubt somebody would soon corner her about the issues the borough had with housing allocation and planning, the increased cost of parking and the poor results in many of the secondary schools. It was the same for all the MPs she knew. She had read through the latest crime statistics, which showed a decrease in theft and violent crime, to provide a more positive vibe, whilst hoping the burgeoning gang culture would not be raised. Although the party in government was far removed from the socialist politics on show tonight, Cheryl had always been on the far left of the party and as such, her appearance appeared to have been accepted by the majority of the audience. However, the other reason she had attended was that, although she was trying to deny it, she had started to sense a strong mutual attraction between herself and Paul.

Looking towards the stage, she could see the main protagonists arriving to sit behind the two ancient trestle tables, covered in marks from old paint and tape. No expense spared then, she thought to herself; they looked like they'd been dragged out of a scout hut. Maybe somebody's idea of "shabby chic", she thought to herself. Put them in a trendy bar in Hoxton and you might get away with it. To either side were large display boards with posters from a range of socialist publications that had organised the event. Cheryl felt the whole impression given was one of totalitarian bleakness. Colours were muted and conversations were serious; there appeared to be no hint of joviality and back slapping that she so much despised witnessing amongst her Cabinet colleagues. An older woman, who she guessed was a trade union representative, was talking animatedly to a group of people in their early twenties. Cheryl was thinking how much it looked like student union hustings, when Paul arrived to sit in the chair next to her. Agile and light-footed, she had hardly heard him as he glided over.

'Hi!' He smiled at her. 'You okay, what do you think? It's a good turnout. Lots of potential supporters for you.' He bowed his head in mock deference.

'Of course, Paul.' Cheryl smiled, knowingly. She could smell his aftershave, a hint of musk and lemon. 'As I said to you before we arrived, I want to attend, but just low key. I am happy to chat a little to some of the constituents, but I can't be seen to be taking the platform,' she said firmly. 'That would be political suicide. I would never be taken seriously as a mainstream politician again.' She looked intently at him. 'You do realise that, don't you?'

'Of course, of course.' Paul nodded earnestly, making a brushing gesture with his hand. 'I quite understand. I was just chatting to several of the local party organisers who have also come along. Your name came up, of course. In fact, it was the first topic of conversation.' He smiled gleefully.

'Go on!' Cheryl raised her eyes. 'Let me guess. A moan fest about the inability of the elected government to fulfil its manifesto promises once elected and how out of touch it now is with local party members.'

'Pretty much. They like you though,' he added enthusiastically. 'We all like what you are doing. It's great to still have somebody who relates to the rank and file and yet holds down a position in the Cabinet.' He smiled at her.

'Thanks, Paul. That means a lot.' She touched his hand gently as it lay on his lap. He looked down and then back at her.

'You know what we need is you in charge, in number ten. Much better all round than the present cock-up. Even the die-hards are noticing the lack of movement on implementing policy.'

'That will never happen, Paul. There are too many middle-of-the-road politicians blocking the path ahead of me. You know that as well as I do!' Cheryl replied. 'Apologies, for the unintentional pun!'

'You never know.' Paul laughed lightly. 'You never know.' He smiled knowingly as he nodded his head.

As Cheryl looked away and sipped a little more of her coffee, he turned around quickly and offered a thumbs up gesture to a man standing behind them. The man nodded back earnestly in acknowledgement. Paul turned back; the plan looked set.

***

Bryan whistled cheerfully as he headed down the winding path that led to the marshes, his faithful border terrier trotting beside him, panting somewhat under the weight of a sprouting coat in urgent need of stripping in the heat of the approaching summer. The light blue sky had just a few puffy white clouds, draped like a cloak over the sea, which was at low tide and stretched out into the distance, laying the numerous rock pools bare. It certainly looked picture postcard perfect, Bryan thought. He waved to their neighbours, already wading knee deep in cold water, tightly holding the hands of their grandchildren, as the two little girls dunked their fishing nets between the rocks, each using a free hand. A few locals he knew from drinking on the benches outside The Coastguard pub nodded over to him. He waved back. He was tempted to join them, but it was just a bit too early, maybe later perhaps. This was the life he had dreamed of for himself and Bunty. A coastal idyll away from the madding crowd. At this time of year, he couldn't think of anywhere else he'd rather be.

Once he was far enough away from their shop and had checked Bunty had not followed him, he took out his burner mobile and looked for any new messages. To his relief, there were none. He put the phone back in his jacket pocket, ready to hide in a place where he hoped Bunty would not find it. Fortunately, she was never over fussy; indeed, if anything, she was messier than he was, with Bryan often finding used coffee cups and plates sprinkled with biscuit crumbs littered around the home. He only used this for his counter intelligence work, which was very occasionally now, given his advancing years.

'Pick it up, mate!'

He was drawn back to reality by a young man holding the hand of a toddler, who was pointing indignantly to a spot beside the path. Looking down, Bryan saw the small dog had just done its business on the patchy grass verge. Raising a hand in acknowledgement, he dutifully picked up the mess. Usually, he thought to himself, the dog was intelligent enough to find a spot off the beaten track, where he could flick it into the undergrowth with a stick if nobody was in close vicinity. Sadly, not today. As the terrier trotted along with a new spring in its step, Bryan made his way along the coastal path to the next available bin a few hundred yards away.

CHAPTER TEN

Penny makes a discovery

When she finally woke up later that morning, Penny was shocked to find it was nearly midday. How long had she slept? Sitting on the small bench on the patio overlooking the vista that spread out below, she munched through a large bowl of muesli and sipped a strong black coffee, brewed in a percolator she had found at the back of a kitchen cupboard. The brisk sea air made it a cool morning and the strong smell of the wood smoke she could see rising from the chimneys confirmed the gentrification of many of the fishermen's cottages. Only recently she had read in a Sunday supplement that wood burners were the first thing installed by most new home owners, and it looked like it was the same for second homes. The peace and quiet was broken by the sound of thumping bass from a car stereo as it passed along the lane below. Just as Penny was beginning to think she was back on her London side street, a car screeched to a halt at the bottom of the hill and she heard loud Cornish voices as the occupants chatted to a group of fishermen. Five minutes later and all she could hear were seagulls, hovering over the patio once more. Clearly, the neighbour had abandoned her shotgun this morning.

Inside her head she was still trying to put the pieces together from her findings as she read through the handwritten notes on the paper beside her.

Findings

Postcard: Hope to see you at the party tomorrow! Don't forget your cowboy outfit and gun. Nikolai.

Letter: Dear Neddy, please can you say hello to my friends. We are all going to the Sea Life centre in Devon this week for my birthday. I think we will have a blast. Thank you, Nikolai Johnson.

Email 1: Nik says thank you to all his friends for the necklace.

Email 2: Present found in unchecked place. N. Johnson. (NECKLACE)

Below she added the following questions:

Who sent the postcard, letter and emails?

What happened at the Devon Sea Life centre?

Who is Nikolai Johnson?

What is the relevance of the necklace?

Retreating back into the cottage, Penny checked the front of both the envelope and the postcard for any evidence of the sender. Although there was no return address, there was the same post office mark from an unspecified area of Kent. She made a note to check this further at the local post office in the town later.

Looking at the emails she had printed out, she saw they had both been sent from the same email address: nikojohnson735@gmail.com. Finally, she switched on her laptop and checked details of the Devon Sea Life bomb blast from several years ago.

There was a large amount of coverage, from both the local and national press, detailing the incident. As Penny read on, several key points appeared from the reporting. It had happened near the end of the day, so less people were in the aquarium at the time. This struck Penny as strange. Surely you would target a busier time for maximum impact. As it turned out, the only people in the centre at the time were a couple of keepers and one family group, consisting of an older couple, their daughter and her two children. Strangely, not all the coverage gave the names of those killed, namely the family and one of the keepers. However, Penny checked the report in the local newspaper, *The Devon Daily.* This gave the married couple as Leonard and Judith Gant, their daughter Julia and her children Peter and Thomas.

Despite using various search engines, she found little more, other than the family had lived in a sleepy suburb of Taunton at the time of the bombing. An extensive image search returned just a single photograph showing a family group standing in a cramped and unkempt back garden, the two children proudly smiling at the camera in their school uniform, in front of a doting mother. First day at school, Penny thought – always a photo opportunity for any parent. There was also an older couple in the background, with a tatty wooden fence as the backdrop. It looked like they were in their early sixties, both fit and trim. The wife was smiling, but the man's face was partly turned away from the camera, as if he had decided not to take part in the photograph at the last minute. Strange, Penny thought to herself. It was as if he didn't want to be photographed for some reason.

There was no mention at all of Nikolai Johnson on the internet. Basically, he didn't appear to exist anywhere. There was no record of any activity listing his name, not even any images. Abandoning any further searches for the time being, Penny shut the lid of the laptop. Instead, she made a coffee and flicked through the free paper that she had found in the letter box at the foot of the garden steps. There was little here to help her search; most pages were full of adverts. A few paragraphs outlined some key up-and-coming events, but there was no mention of Stewart's death.

***

After lunch, Penny felt alert enough to venture down to the post office, despite so little sleep. She remembered seeing the sign outside the convenience store she had visited the day before for provisions. Inside, there was just one person at the small counter in the corner, which was separate from the main aisles. As she moved forward to be served, she was relieved to see the man she had spoken to before, who had introduced himself as Mr Shah, the shop owner, behind the glass partition.

'Hello again!' Penny smiled brightly. 'I wonder if you can help me. I have these two items of correspondence and I am trying to trace where they were sent from.' She handed over the letter and the postcard. 'I can see it was Kent, but I wondered if you could be more specific than that?' she added, smiling her best smile as he took them.

'Let me see.' The man turned to his side and typed a few keystrokes into a computer, humming to himself as he did so. The shop was obviously quiet at this time of day. In a few seconds, it was clear he had a response on the screen. 'Yes, I can tell you from the unique number on the postmark that they were sent from the small sub-post office at St Margaret's at Cliffe.'

'Great, thanks!' Smiling again, she left the shop.

Penny walked back up the hill deep in thought. What was her next move? She had just settled into the cottage and purchased enough provisions to stay for a few more days. The break was just what she needed and there was plenty here to keep her occupied. At the same time, she knew she needed to get to the bottom of Stewart's death and this seemed a good lead to follow. After all, that was the reason she had come down here in the first place. By the time she had reached the front door and checked her watch, her mind was made up. It took her a few minutes to pick up the few personal items she needed. If she left and got the train now, she could get back to London this evening. Tomorrow she would drive out to Kent, in the hope of getting some answers to her list of questions.

PART THREE

SURVEILLANCE

CHAPTER ELEVEN

The railway exhibition

Jesse checked the phone once more as he was drinking a second strong coffee. Using Google Maps he could see it was a fairly accessible location, just over two miles from the M40: along a chalk ridge and through one small village before skirting the top of the hill and past the windmill he had been to the last time. That had been fairly straightforward really. He had been given the combination and within a minute he had removed the package and closed the small door below the letterbox in the front wall. As he looked across the small room, he could see the package, still unopened as per instructions, waiting for his attention under a pile of clothes on the small foam sofa. This time he had to continue down the hill and then turn right into the small village. There was adequate parking beside the pub, but it was probably best to leave the bike outside the entrance to the village hall, where the exhibition was being held. That way he would be guaranteed a fast exit and should be out of the village in under a minute.

He looked at his watch. The exhibition was due to start at noon. He certainly didn't want to be early. He only intended to be in the place for a short period of time, just long enough to make the switch. Perhaps arrive just after one p.m. when most visitors have arrived. That meant leaving in half an hour. On the table was the model he had purchased with next day delivery as part of a set that also included track and a controller. He had no use for any of it other than the one piece. He removed the tender and placed it in the small cardboard box he had also ordered, which would hold it safely within the pannier of his motorcycle.

***

As Dom woke, it dawned on him once again that he would not be spending this Saturday in his usual preferred way. He would not be walking into town to meet his mates at their favourite pub, a small tap room attached to a microbrewery that produced a wide selection of wonderful real ales. His mouth salivated as he thought of the drinks he would be missing. He would also not be walking the half a mile to watch the Wycombe Wanderers home game with an even larger group of mates, followed by a walk back to another pub and a long post-match analysis chat over more drinks, which may lead to eating somewhere nearby with his partner. No, he would not be doing any of this. Instead, he would be going to a railway exhibition, with a man who most of his colleagues shunned, on the pretence of interest, but with the intention of reuniting with an old friend who he had not spoken to for ten years and who he probably now had nothing in common with.

Dom closed his eyes and lay on his back. How on earth had it come to this? Why could he not just accept his lot? True, it was relatively mundane, but many would envy the lifestyle of a lecturer, albeit of rather limited-ability language students, living in a pleasant dormitory town, surrounded by unspoilt countryside and brimming with independent amenities that kept the chattering classes happy. No, instead he had jumped at the chance to carry out covert work for his country. Indeed, to become a secret agent. A spy. And a grubby little spy at that. Turning in the king size bed, he saw his partner, Fay, had already woken, and the noise from below indicated that both the dog and the morning cup of tea were both being attended to.

'Who are you playing today?' she asked brightly, with her usual enthusiasm, as she handed him the warm mug.

'Brentford, strong side, they're heading for promotion. Not sure if we stand much of a chance.' He had thought it best to not mention his actual plans. Later, when asked, he would produce the story that he had had to give Gerry a lift at the last minute and had then missed the match, getting lost in the country lanes on the way back. There was always an issue parking near the ground and the fact that he had the car would give him the excuse not to go drinking.

'Usual crowd going today?'

'Yes, hopefully,' he said breezily, attempting fake enthusiasm. 'Anyway, what are your plans?'

'A few of the girls from work are coming over to walk the dogs. We thought we might drive out to one of the Chiltern villages and take a picnic.'

'What!' He reddened. Let's hope to God it's not the same one, he thought. Recovering his composure, he replied, 'Sorry, of course a great idea. Get some fresh air.'

'Yes, we thought so. A nice chance to catch up. Maybe we'll visit a pub. Kaz said she visited a lovely old one a few weeks ago.'

Dom drank his tea thoughtfully. Some of his plan may need some careful rearranging.

***

'I didn't know you liked model railways?' said Shona, genuinely shocked.

They were heading out into the Chiltern countryside for a pub lunch. The sun shone across the green fields, scattered with grazing sheep. It was a short fifteen-minute drive and they were soon passing The Cow and

Butcher and parking opposite the village green. She was surprised Dima had insisted on leaving so early, just after ten o'clock, especially as she had closed the shop for the first Saturday since a friend's wedding, nearly a year ago. Shona had been looking forward to a repeat of the previous night's lovemaking. Instead, they were both in hiking gear, ready to take in a long walk before they had lunch.

To be honest, Shona was dreading what was beginning to resemble a formidable march. Yes, it all looked lovely and the footpaths that led across the fields were littered with small copses. Yes, it was bucolic, but surely Dima had countryside like this back home, she thought. Still, she consoled herself with the prospect of a well-earned meal and the pub did have excellent reviews – she had checked this as soon as he told her of their destination. Time was precious, as she remembered from their last meeting several years ago. It could all end so quickly. That was the nature of Dima's work, whatever that was. She was never quite sure to be honest.

'It's no big deal. I'll nip in now before we go for the walk. It's just up the path there.' He waved a hand in the general direction of the church. 'I just want to show a locomotive at the exhibition. It's rare, so people may be interested. I don't need to wait. We can pick it up later.' He smiled at her. With that, he turned and headed off up the narrow lane, humming to himself as he went.

Shona yawned as she waited by the car, glancing casually at the church notice board beside the village green. There was a flyer for the exhibition behind the glass cover and she could see it was due to begin in half an hour. Shona could not imagine anyone being interested in a load of trains. Surely this was the type of thing men stopped thinking about once they ceased to be little boys. God, she thought, I couldn't stand being stuck with an old man who spent all his time in a garden shed or the loft playing with his train set. She looked at Dima as he walked out of sight, dressed rather like an action man. Now she came to think of it, he did look quite a bit older than his previous visit. His stubble was darker, his eyebrows thicker, and wasn't that hair protruding from his ears? The already thin hair appeared to have retreated further and a monk's bald patch was clearly visible from behind. Still, there was no problem in the bedroom; there were certainly no complaints in that department. Shona smiled to herself. She would have to generate some other interests that were more mainstream and, more importantly, that they could share together.

A couple of hours later, and they had finished a picturesque three-mile trek, taking in the windmill perched on the hill ridge and two of the neighbouring villages. They had even stopped for a drink in one of them, Dima insisting on tasting a pint of the local Brakspear real ale, brewed in nearby Henley-on-

Thames. Now as they descended the final few yards of the footpath, completing the circular walk, her car came into sight once more.

'Come on, let's have a spot of lunch.' He took her hand and they entered the low-ceilinged bar. Inside, the pub was as rustic as its exterior, but was clearly an upmarket eating establishment. Shona's spirits rose. Fortunately, he had rung ahead and booked a small table by the window, which looked suitably romantic with a small vase of wildflowers. Sparing no expense, he ordered a bottle of good French red wine and planned his next move as Shona intently studied the expensive menu.

***

As Gerry did not possess a car, Dom had arranged to drive them to the show and arrived at the pre-arranged time of eleven thirty outside the flat. Gerry had been insistent that he wanted to arrive as soon as it opened, so Dom was somewhat surprised that he was kept waiting for a further ten minutes on the double yellow lines, checking regularly for any sign of a traffic warden in his side-view mirrors. When he did arrive, Gerry looked flustered. The reason why soon became apparent when Dom spotted a surly-looking boy of mid-teenage years in a hoodie and loose-fitting tracksuit bottoms shuffling in the background. In contrast, Gerry seemed to be wearing his usual work clothes, namely a tweed jacket and a pair of old black suit trousers, with the trademark low-slung crutch. His one concession to a casual look were a pair of bright white trainers, which were either unused or a relatively new purchase.

'Hi, Dom. Sorry for the delay. I was waiting for Josh, my neighbour's kid. Okay if he comes along?' Gerry's voice trailed off, as he saw Dom glaring back.

The boy raised his hooded head and nodded a passing acknowledgement to Dom, before opening the rear door and seating himself on the back seat. Great! Immediately Dom felt his stress levels rising as he heard the loud rap beat emitting at a loud level from the boy's contactless headphones, hidden inside the depths of his hood. Hope he blasts his bloody eardrums, Dom thought to himself. Gerry was already seated next to him in the passenger seat, cradling a large supermarket bag for life on his lap. As he looked, Dom was sure some of the shapes pushing through the thin plastic distinctly resembled tubs of pot noodles.

'Got some provisions to keep us going.' He tapped the bag. 'And a few items to show,' he said, as he saw Dom looking at the bag. He was barely able to contain his excitement; clearly this was a highlight of Gerry's social calendar.

'Show?' Dom repeated.

'Yes, there is always a stand where anyone can bring in rare or interesting locomotives and rolling stock. It gives you a chance to show them to other modellers,' Gerry replied.

'Show off?' Dom tried not to laugh.

'No.' Gerry was adamant. 'Oh no, not "show off". Never!' Gerry looked taken aback and was clearly hurt by the insinuation. 'It's all about sharing each other's experiences. It's about being supportive of other modellers in our community.'

Dom nodded to himself. This could well be the handover location. It certainly fitted. It could almost be the classic music case left on a seat at the opera, or the left luggage locker.

As the car travelled the fifteen miles or so due west to the location of the show, the fact that Gerry had not applied much, if any, deodorant became increasingly apparent. The sun was shining and despite Dom opening the window a little and mouth breathing as much as possible, the musty smell quickly began to fill the small space. He tried to lower it further, but changed his mind as the cold air rushed in. As soon as they arrived at the village and had parked, both Dom and Josh had exited the car instantly, leaving a somewhat bemused Gerry trudging behind them up the steps to the village hall, mumbling under his breath. Dom kept his collar up and his head down as he sprinted ahead, hoping Fay and her friends had chosen another location.

'Wait for me lads!' Gerry called out, wrongly sensing a form of camaraderie. 'You need these.' He waved the tickets above his head. Dom checked his watch – 11:50. An elderly woman, who was knitting as she sat behind a small desk, glared at them defiantly and then pointed to a sign that stated in bold print: "NOON OPENING". To reinforce her point, she toothlessly mouthed the words silently to them.

Five minutes later and they were inside. Dom had resisted the temptation, and it was tempting, to give a single middle finger to the officious woman. Instead, both he and Josh had stood back, while Gerry delivered what Dom could only describe as a bizarre form of geek flirting. It worked. Having bamboozled her with technical jargon, Gerry clinched the deal with the offer of a pickled onion pot noodle later. She melted and waved them through as they handed over their tickets, all initial hostilities forgotten. The small entrance corridor led down to a pair of double doors. Standard layout for a small Victorian village hall, Dom noted. Inside the main room were two massive railway layouts. He knew enough to know that these both appeared to be 00 gauge and were likely to be precision representations of actual railways. He remembered Gerry had explained that modellers often prided themselves on the obscure locations they chose to recreate. Dom was impressed with the way the layouts had been positioned to allow maximum access to view all parts of the models, whilst allowing space for walkways through the room – this was clearly a professional job.

Within a few minutes, Gerry had left their side and was in deep conversation with the couple working on one of the exhibits – a scale model of the Great Western Railway from Exeter to Penzance, running along the Devon and Cornwall coastline. Several locomotives pulled carriages along the tracks through tunnels and over viaducts, before arriving at the detailed mainline stations, disappearing into sidings or onto the turntables. Dom had to admit the level of workmanship was extremely impressive. He noticed that Josh had disappeared to the end of the room away from all models and was nodding his head to the beat in his headphones. Presumably the trip was just an opportunity to remove him from his family for a short period of respite.

With less than ten people in the large room, it was clear that Dima was not present. Dom moved around the exhibition to take in the second model, which represented the sidings at a Belgian coastal port, Ostend to be precise.

Gerry was leaning over the only other display area, which Dom took to be the show area. The contents of the plastic bag were now strewn over the floor in front of the large table and Gerry was picking up his models in turn, deciding which warranted being put on display. As Dom approached, it appeared that Gerry had made his decision and was starting to arrange a gleaming red steam locomotive and its brightly painted carriages on the plinth he had been allocated.

‘Queen of the South.’ He stood back and nodded, taking in the model in its position.

‘Great!’ said Dom, trying to appear suitably impressed. ‘Really great!’ he added for emphasis.

‘Thanks, mate. Glad you like it. Means a lot. Let’s see what the visitors think.’ He pointed to a small pile of cards ready for comments from fellow enthusiasts. It struck Dom that the size of the pile suggested the organisers weren’t expecting a particularly large turnout.

Dom had realised that spotting Dima’s arrival was likely to be straightforward. Moving to the only other table, he ordered a cup of tea and a slice of carrot cake from a bored-looking teenager, likely to be the offspring of one of the younger organisers. Indeed, this was confirmed when Dom saw a man of a similar age to himself make his way over and say a few words to the teenager, who in turn scowled and pointed to the time on the large clock above the double doors, clearly feeling he had fulfilled his side of the agreement.

It really would just be a case of positioning himself with a good vantage point and keeping an unobstructed view of the main entrance to the room. Already, he noticed the numbers had increased in the past few minutes, with over twenty, mainly older males, now milling around the displays. As he watched, he saw several of the models next to Gerry’s being carefully picked up and thoroughly examined; it would take very little effort to make a swap, Dom thought to himself. It really was a stroke of genius on Dima's part. He moved over to look at the other models on display beside Gerry's exhibit. One caught his eye. Surely not… Of course, it could be a coincidence. Two rows behind the Queen of the South and at the end of the row, standing proud, was a large black locomotive and tender. Underneath the model in large block writing was a label proclaiming:

The Soviet steam locomotive

4-14-4

Big Boy "Andrey Andreev"

Dom stared. Could it be that Dima had been in and set up this before he had even arrived?

As he was looking thoughtfully at the model, the mobile vibrated in his jacket pocket. It was Tim. He swiped to accept, but the signal was pretty weak and Dom made his way outside to take the call. As he left the building, several more people were now entering. Finding a vacant bench in the corner of the small parking area, he listened as Tim talked animatedly.

'We're in luck. It looks like Dima decided to use the phone we are tapping to send the rendezvous information for the handover.' Tim was clearly checking his messages as he spoke. 'Okay, firstly a photo of a magazine, outlining the railway exhibition location and time – we knew that anyway. Ahh, this is new. Now we have a photo of a steam locomotive,

“Andrey Andreev”. Ring any bells?’ It certainly did. Dom got that sinking feeling. He started to run back towards the entrance.

‘It’s here, on display. I just saw it! I’ll go back inside now.’

‘Wait,’ Tim replied from inside the phone. ‘We’ve got another cryptic clue. I said Dima likes to use them. “Painful from intended error”, six letters apparently. Search me.’

‘Oh, that’s straightforward.’ Dom attempted *The Times* crossword in the senior common room most lunchtimes, to avoid having to chat to most of his colleagues. ‘Some word similar to “pain”, six letters long and made from the letters in the words “intended error”. It’s not the locomotive; it is the tender that will be handed over. Whatever he has brought in, that’s where he has concealed it. I’ll go now and take it.’

He had lowered his voice now he had entered the building, aware of the angry stares from the modellers, who clearly frowned on the use of mobile phones inside the exhibition.

Dom rang off and turned, nearly bumping into a motorcyclist in full black leathers and wearing a helmet, who was heading hurriedly out of the hall. He headed straight for the display, waving aside Gerry who had appeared excitedly by his side, trying to inform Dom that his model had just been awarded “Highly commended”, waving the rosette rather like a child placed at their first gymkhana. In a few bounds, Dom was standing in front of the display. It was with a sense of relief that he saw the model was still there. However, as he looked, he could see something was wrong. Something had changed. On closer inspection, he could see it now. The locomotive was indeed there, the shining black Andrey Andreev, with its large number of wheels. It was the tender that Dom looked at closely. It was not the same. True, it was black and of a similar size, but the letter font and size were very slightly different. It was definitely not the tender he had seen a few minutes earlier.

He turned and ran out of the hall, jumping into his car and hurtling down the small lane, past several disgruntled elderly walkers. Dom knew it was fruitless, but he had to at least make the effort and give chase, before he faced relaying the bad news to Tim. When he reached the end of the lane, he caught a glimpse of the black motorbike disappearing into the distance. It was too far away to read the licence plate. As he turned, he caught sight of a couple leaving the pub in the corner of his eye – her with auburn hair, him looking possibly Eastern European, smartly dressed compared to his companion. His eyes lingered long enough for him to catch the wry smile on Dima's face as he crossed the road and got into the passenger side of a small hatchback.

Leaving the village, he put his foot to the floor of his

car, driving rather like in a computer game, and he began to close in slightly on the motorbike weaving down the lane ahead. Then it was gone. Slowing down, he saw the small entrance to a field on his left, and in that moment, the rider, having spun full circle, shot past his driver's door and left Dom's bulky SUV wallowing in its wake. Within a second it was out of sight completely. Any further chase was clearly pointless.

***

It had worked a treat. A quick detour to lose the car following him and then down the narrow country lanes flanked with high hedges meant Jesse's progress would be virtually untraceable, especially as he intended to use the back road to Henley-on-Thames, rather than the motorway, and thus try to avoid most CCTV opportunities. The small package was safely stored in the pannier behind him. He knew what it contained. Soon he would be given instructions on what to do next with it.

Changing up a gear, he accelerated, picking up more speed as the road widened. His rear-view mirrors reassuringly showed no sign of any further pursuit. The motorcycle purred as he unleashed more of its potential. Soon the road weaved through the dense beech woods, common to the area. Reaching a small empty parking area at the entrance to the Forestry Commission land, he pulled over and dismounted. In less than a minute he had removed the false number plates, ripping off the plastic film to reveal the actual plates underneath. A short walk was all that was needed to hide the plastic inside the small opening of an ancient tree. By the time he had replaced the foliage, it would have been impossible to know the trunk had ever been disturbed. CCTV no longer a problem, he took the most direct route back to the campsite.

***

'Whatever you do, don't touch it!' Tim's voice was clear and shrill.

'Tim? Look, I'm sorry, Tim,' he tried to interrupt.

'Listen,' Tim continued. 'You won't have seen it but today there was a major incident at Heathrow. The scanning mechanisms picked up Novichok in the men's toilet in the arrivals lounge, between customs and immigration. Remember Salisbury? Well, we checked. Our friend Dima was caught on CCTV entering those toilets in an agitated state. Sweating profusely and swaying as he stumbled into them. He must have had a minuscule trace on him and then transferred it to the toilet pan. No wonder the bloody fool felt sick, you would. He must have nearly been a goner. Amazed he is still with us. Must have got a minute amount on his hand or clothes when he placed the stuff inside the model. Very careless. The poor bloody cleaner collapsed and is in intensive care. We've had to gag the national press. Imagine the headlines after Salisbury – they'd have a bloody field day. So be careful with it, Dom.'

'Sorry, Tim, I haven't got it!' There was urgency in Dom's voice now.

'What! What happened? No show. Oh, thank God. He hasn't used it yet. There's still time.' Tim sounded relieved; the fast breathing had stopped. 'What a relief, what a relief!' He repeated himself.

'No.' Dom felt bad, very bad. 'It was in the tender. I came outside to take your call – the reception in that old building was terrible. I returned and it was a different tender on the train. It had been switched in the time I was outside. I gave chase after the motorcyclist, who was the only person leaving, but they got away and I didn't get the full plate, just NH67…' His voice trailed off.

'Christ!' Tim was almost screaming now. 'You mean Dima has brought Novichok into the UK and has transferred it to an unknown agent, who has subsequently disappeared without trace. Jesus! This is a nightmare, Dom. An absolute nightmare!'

With the sound of a phone being thrown down, Tim hung up.

CHAPTER TWELVE

Penny investigates further

One advantage of arriving back to her house at close to midnight, Penny reflected, was that at least the builders had finally stopped working for the day. Not even the neighbours in her gentrified enclave in the London borough could afford to employ them that late, although finishing after seven in the evening and working all weekend now seemed par for the course.

On the train, Penny had a chance to research more about the village of St Margaret's at Cliffe. Bizarrely, it was a good mile inland, presumably stranded on what were now reclaimed marshes. The route on the map app showed that from her home address to the post office should take about an hour. That would at least give her a chance to have some sort of a lie in. The village had a population of under five hundred, suggesting there was unlikely to be a long queue. She decided not to ring ahead – much better to turn up and inquire casually. After all, as Penny reminded herself, she was not part of any official investigation.

As she opened the front door, she saw a large brown envelope fall from where it was suspended precariously on the inside ledge of the letterbox. Penny recognised the writing instantly. Her suspicions were confirmed when she opened it and found the third draft of a contract she had negotiated on behalf of one of her clients for a role in a new TV series. So much for the office taking care of her workload! The truth was, she missed her job and was beginning to feel anxious about the progress of her clients' work and careers. Penny signed it and then decided to post it back tomorrow. She would do it at the post office; it would provide an extra element to her cover story.

***

In fact, once Penny had started driving the next day, it was clear she was travelling against the main traffic flow and was likely to arrive a little early. She dropped a disc into the CD player. The first track brought a tear to her eye as she thought once more of Stewart, smiling back at her over a glass of rosé at one of their many restaurant liaisons. Soon the motorway was a distant memory and the car travelled along a single-track road that wound along a chalk ridge, interspersed with sheep and large rounded hay bales that lay like great organic boulders on the farmland. Penny checked the temperature gauge regularly as the car had a history of overheating, but to her relief it stayed out of the red zone.

As the last notes faded out, she found herself entering the village. It was functional rather than picturesque, more bungalows and open-plan lawns than quaint cottages with picket fences. This is more Cornwall than Cotswolds, Penny thought to herself. More importantly, it possessed a small car park in the centre, just off the main road through it. Despite this clearly being the main parking facility for many locals, Penny managed to find a rather tight space to ease into beside the toilet block, which, much to her annoyance, was currently out of order. Walking out of the car park, she found the post office sign almost opposite on a deserted narrow street. The sky was cloudless and there was no sign here of any seagulls, unlike her time in Cornwall.

As she opened the newly painted door and stepped down into the shop, a metallic bell clanked and a small, slightly dumpy, bookish-looking woman came out from the back room and smiled broadly from across the counter. The large round glasses framing her eyes gave her a reassuring owl-like appearance, which was topped off with a tight bun haircut. The main shop itself struck Penny as a rather over-cluttered area, with a variety of local products competing with each other for customer attention from the stands located around the walls. A faded brown cork notice board beside the counter contained a plethora of business cards, giving the place the feel of a community hub. There was a large cardboard box on the front desk with a handwritten sign in black marker pen: "Items for next post – next collection 4:30 p.m." She dropped the envelope holding the contract into it and then made her way over to the main counter to address the woman, who was still smiling and looked at her expectantly. As Penny stepped forward, she pulled out the letter and postcard from the inside pocket of her waxed jacket.

'Hi, I am trying to find out any information about these?' She passed over the letter and the postcard. 'I understand from inquiries made to the post office helpline that they were sent from this post office. From the number on the postmark, I think.'

The woman held the two items close to her eyes, moving the glasses further down her nose, as she carefully studied each postmark in turn.

'Yes, that's true. But these were sent several years ago. In fact, about ten years ago looking at the dates,' she replied.

'Were you here then?' Penny asked.

'Well, yes, but we can't remember who posts the items. Just the few regulars. And we have had quite a lot of incomers into the village since we first arrived here.' It struck Penny that the woman now seemed a little flustered. 'It would be nearly impossible to search back through the records to find information on the senders of these,' the woman continued.

'Ah. Well, you can see they both appear to come from the same person, Nikolai Johnson. Does anybody of that name live around here or use the post office on a regular basis?'

Was she imagining it or did Penny see the woman take a sharp intake of breath before shaking her head slowly? 'No, we don't have anybody of that name using this place.'

'Well, thanks.' Penny turned to go. 'Just one more thing. Does anything to do with a necklace mean anything to you?'

The woman shook her head again.

'No. Sorry I can't be of any help.'

As Penny went to leave, an active-looking man in his late sixties with a small terrier dog who had just entered the shop smiled and stood back to let her pass. Walking out, Penny pointed to the jewellery display beside the door by a local artist.

'I don't suppose the necklace reference has anything to do with these?' She laughed.

***

'Are you all right? You look like you've seen a ghost.' A concerned Bryan walked towards the counter, the terrier trotting obediently by his side.

'I'll be fine, Bryan. It's just one of my funny turns.

I get them these days. With my age, remember?'

Bryan nodded. He remembered the lecture he had been given the other night when he had awoken freezing with no duvet on the bed. Bunty had given him a detailed ten-minute resume of her problems with night sweats. Wisely, he kept his mouth firmly shut this time.

'Keep an eye out here while I make a cuppa and have a sit down, will you love?' she continued.

With that, Bunty turned away and moved quickly through to the back room to put the kettle on before Bryan could answer. She had to let Dima know. Asking about Nikolai Johnson and even mentioning the necklace – this had never happened before. Bunty felt her heart pounding. And in front of Bryan! Thankfully he knew nothing about any of it. Thank God he was blissfully ignorant on that score. She took out the burner mobile and lit a cigarette, her first for over a week. She knew Bryan hated her smoking, which gave her the excuse to disappear up the back garden with the phone. If he did come out, he would see the smoke and wrongly assume this to be the reason for her covert trip outside. Climbing the concrete slabs up the steep bank and settling on the plastic garden chair beside the potting shed, Bunty knew she would see Bryan if he approached, the only entrance being through a gap in the laurel hedge that segregated the main garden from this small end section.

She sent the one word, "Necklace", followed by an

emoji of a woman. It would be enough for Dima. He would be able to track the woman. Hesitating, Bunty wondered whether she should have sent more information, but decided against it. She realised she had not checked if the woman had a car and got the registration. More importantly, she had failed to check the details of where the letter and postcard had been sent. That would have given her location. But of course, Dima would know this. After all, it was he who sent them to that TV presenter.

Afterwards, she smashed the mobile and battery separately, having taken out the SIM card. On the way back down the steps, she placed the SIM card in the middle of the food waste bin and threw the two parts of the case in different directions far into the woodland that bordered the east side of their garden. It was overgrown and the farmer had not been seen entering this part of his ground for well over a year. By the time she had returned to the shop, Bunty had fully composed herself.

***

He stared at the mobile. Clearly something was up. The codeword was only sent to him if there was a problem, a big problem. The burner number matched one of those he had given to Bunty – dropped off at a left luggage locker at St Pancras International station by another agent under his orders a couple of years ago. Dima trusted Bunty implicitly. She was his longest running agent. In fact, she had been active before he came on the scene, having been in contact with his predecessor. Her involvement had always been logistics, communications to be precise. Hence the post office. It was a perfect connection in an age when security services monitored everything sent by every possible media. It had been a stroke of genius really. And then it had worked so well, almost hidden in plain sight. Particularly when passing information for the killing of that traitor and his family at the Sea Life centre. Like himself, he knew that Bunty had felt no anguish over the deaths. To them both, betrayal was the ultimate. No way back. True, the killings of his relatives had been unfortunate and he knew that Bunty had agonised slightly over the unfortunate death of the zookeeper. He had to admit, he had felt the same himself.

And then more recently, that gullible TV presenter had read out the messages! An official channel in the Motherland couldn't have done a better job. And nobody knew. It was perfect. Even thinking about it now made him smile at its simplicity. Nothing had been traced back to the Necklace agents at all. He had chosen the codename Necklace. It was back in Moscow, meeting Britzchov, his own controller, that he remembered his own words well. He had been sitting across the desk from his old mentor in a smart office.

'Yes, I am pleased,' he had said. 'I have recruited

excellent agents. Each operative is a pearl. And I control the ring. The spy ring. In fact, I think I may use the codename Necklace for the spy ring. For a ring of pearls, you see.'

Britzchov had nodded. 'I rather like that. And of course, an easy throw away if any issues develop.' He lowered his voice. They both knew: interrogation techniques always pushed for the key words.

And now the fool had gone and spilled the beans. He hadn't meant to. It was accidental of course; he didn't even know what he had been doing. He had been an unwilling accomplice to the plan, but still an integral part. But he had unknowingly said too much and they couldn't risk any further leaks. They'd had to silence Stewart. And now Bunty had picked up something. Something serious. He placed the phone back in the back pocket of his jeans as Shona came through to the lounge with two cups of coffee and a plate of digestive biscuits. The next step would take some serious thought.

CHAPTER THIRTEEN

Consequences

Dom was wading through an attempt at marking yet more substandard work in his shed, when the message came through on his amateur radio set. Since the disaster of the previous day, he had been keeping a low profile, for once even trying to immerse himself in his work, although he was finding this a harder task than he had imagined. After losing the motorcycle, he had returned crestfallen to the village hall and tried to prise Gerry away from the exhibition, which was close to finishing anyway. He realised that he had missed the football match, but there was just a chance he may be able to meet up with the rest of his mates at the pub afterwards. There was no such luck however, as once he had managed to get Gerry to leave, they spent a further half an hour trying to find his neighbour's annoying teenage son. Eventually, Gerry spotted him walking around the churchyard chatting on his phone. It wasn't so bad. Dom had just about made the last few rounds and then they had managed to get a table at a favourite restaurant. In fact, he had been ecstatic just to see the back of Gerry and his bloody neighbour.

So now he was working in the shed, glass of red in hand, waiting to see if Tim called him with an update. He felt it was the least he could do. After all, he had been asked to carry out a fairly simple task and he had failed. Indeed, he had failed quite spectacularly. And of course, the message came through just before five o'clock that Sunday. Usual place, usual time.

***

Later that evening in Tim's study, it had become apparent to Dom that the departure of Marcus to carry out surveillance had left its mark – domesticity had appeared to have all but broken down. As he had been led through the house this time, he noted the dirty patches on the carpets, presumably soiled after muddy dog walks, and caught a fleeting glimpse of the unwashed plates piled up in the kitchen. Dom had already noticed the overflowing landfill bin, parked askew on the front drive when he arrived.

The whisky was a new bottle – never a good sign – and was already two thirds empty. How much had Tim drunk in the few days since their last meeting, Dom asked himself. Aware that he had been responsible for a gross error of judgement in letting the tender out of his sight, he decided to keep these thoughts to himself. The smell of dog seemed stronger than ever, but thankfully the heating system seemed to have settled at a sensible ambient temperature. His craving for a cigarette was becoming stronger and he was painfully aware he had finished the last of his pack of gum a few hours ago.

'It appears we have a possible lead.' Tim's opening gambit was more positive than Dom had been expecting, namely furrowed brows, a thunderous temper and a dressing down. In fact, he had been ready to call it a day, rather than listen to a detailed outline of all his inadequacies.

'Really? That's great news, Tim!' Dom instantly felt more at ease.

'Yes, do you remember the codename Necklace? It was several years back now. We had strong suspicions back then that it was a Russian spy ring, led by either Dima or another controller.'

'Vaguely. How long ago?'

'Hard to say. It was never linked to anything in particular, such as the Salisbury or Devon events. But the name Necklace came up at the time from one of our operatives. Now it has come up again. One of our agents who is now retired runs a little post office in a sleepy seaside village in Kent. He has contacted us to say a middle-aged woman was in his shop asking about the necklace, apparently sent on some emails she had received.'

‘How strange. Was she an agent of the Motherland, one of Dima’s gang?’

‘Hardly, unless she was performing a very brash double bluff. No, according to our contact, this was very genuine, an innocent inquiry.’

‘So, a dead end?’ said Dom, struggling to see the relevance of this new information.

‘Not exactly. He was smart enough to get her car number as she drove off. Our techies have tracked it to a Penny Grainger, an agent at a London media agency. Starzer Associates. Lives in North West London with her partner.’

‘Okay. So we traced her I suppose?’ Dom perked up at the news.

‘Yes.’ Tim smiled as he took another sip. ‘And we checked who she represents. A mixture of authors and media personalities, some we’d never heard of to be honest. Only one thing came out. Do you remember that faded TV presenter who was killed in a mugging outside a TV studio in London last month?’

Dom racked his brain. ‘Not really.’ He tended to avoid anything that involved the concept of celebrity and in his opinion, television personalities fell into that category. If truth be known, he prided himself in being rather an academic snob.

‘Well, she used to represent him before he retired,’ Tim said triumphantly.

‘Not much of a link, is it?’ To Dom, it seemed like a

dead end.

'Well, we need to have full surveillance on her. Flat out for a week. Do you fancy it?'

Tim pulled his most persuasive face. It sounded appealing. A week away from those dreaded Russian lectures, away from the university and the weak-willed students. And his dreaded boss. A week under the radar and away from the constant rigorous accountability he so loathed. It may be just what he needed. Not to mention the kudos he would feel being fully operational, even if he couldn't share this with any colleagues. Then reality set in and the undeniable fact that he would return to an even larger stack of marking. Not to mention the covertness of it all. Dom shook his head.

'Thanks for keeping me in the loop. And for the offer. But now is not the right time.'

Tim nodded and then shrugged his shoulders as he continued.

'I thought you would say that. Don't worry, I have a back-up option. I may still need to call on you for a one off, if needed.'

'Fine, Tim,' Dom replied. 'That's fine, of course.'

Secretly hoping he would not be required to deliver on the promise, Dom downed the remainder of the whisky before he was allocated a more demanding task. As he stood up, he saw Tim had already poured himself another whisky and had started on a new game of patience.

CHAPTER FOURTEEN

An unwelcome approach

Cheryl looked at her expensive, gold watch for the fourth time in the last minute. It was now approaching nine o'clock. She ran her fingers through her hair. The glass of pinot grigio was already almost empty and she had resisted the temptation of the free peanuts and crisps that had also arrived, instead nibbling on some thin rye crispbread, trying to convince herself they tasted just as good. The bar, like so many in the area, was at the front of a small boutique Soho hotel. Her seat was by the window, with her legs tucked under the narrow table ledge that ran the whole length of the front wall.

The relatively attractive middle-aged man, who had smiled at her and raised his glass of red wine when she arrived, was still sitting in the leather club armchair beside the fireplace flicking through his phone. She could tell he was casually watching her. Around them, the walls and ceiling of the bar were lined with old theatre and opera house posters. Cheryl would have loved to have browsed them, but she wanted to avoid the attention of the man. Instead, she people-watched the street outside as tourists and night workers mingled down the narrow lane. It was easy to spot the difference: the slow drifting from shop front to bar window, compared to the purposeful stride and quickened step. The light began to fade as the evening set in, leaving the diners in the restaurant opposite framed in by spotlights in the windows as they ate. Cheryl was drawn away from her thoughts by a cough, and she turned to find the barman standing next to her.

'The gentleman wishes to buy you a drink.' The barman nodded his head subtly in the direction of the fireplace. Cheryl looked around. The bar was otherwise empty and the man raised his glass and smiled back, inviting her to join him. He really was quite dishy in the subtle lighting. She looked at her watch; it was now quarter past nine. When she had accepted the invitation, this had been the one concern at the back of her mind. Namely, being approached or chatted up, whilst she was waiting on her own.

'Err…' She cleared her throat, as the man once more smiled over. 'Tell the gentleman thank you, but…' Her voice trailed off as Paul arrived, just in time, bounding into the bar, apologising for his lateness. She imagined he could see the relief in her eyes as she pecked his cheek and held his arm.

'Of course, madam. Of course,' said the barman,

nodded knowingly as he retreated, followed by Paul ordering himself a large glass of malbec.

A few minutes later, Cheryl looked past Paul and saw the empty armchair. The man had already left the bar. What she had not seen was the acknowledgement he had received from Paul as he left.

CHAPTER FIFTEEN

Awake and monitoring

Asimov rolled over in the large futon bed and rearranged himself, continuing his sleep. He had taken most of the duvet. Tanya was awake anyway. She looked at his perfect features in side profile. Thick black hair swept back from his smooth skin, framing his classic high cheekbones and chiselled jawline. Even his snoring was mild and rhythmic. Totally bearable, and indeed, somewhat reassuring. He could have been an android created as a perfect man.

It was just before dawn and the open window signalled that for once, the city was quiet, not yet fully back to life. At this time, the air seemed free from the heavy acrid taste of pollution, Tanya thought, as the cool breeze that reached her face was perfumed by the pines that grew abundantly around the edge of the city. Just a short period of calm for the senses, before the inevitable onslaught that heralded the start of the early morning rush hour. Turning onto her side with her back to him, she took a swig from the bottle of mineral water, before picking up the mobile from the bedside table and opening her messages. A final check reassured her that Asimov was still asleep.

'Just requesting an update and any further instructions?'

She sent the text and lay back waiting for the reply. About ten minutes later the phone vibrated once, indicating the new message had arrived. Still Asimov dozed peacefully beside her.

'Target is fully operational. You will be sent details regarding your departure in the next day.'

She smiled and switched the phone off. A few minutes later, Asimov stirred, getting up to use the en suite toilet. He glided catlike across the floor, hardly making a sound. As he returned, he was wider awake and pulled back the duvet, revealing Tanya's brief nightdress. She could see he was ready to make love, his eyes eagerly taking in her body as she lay back. Touching his lips with her forefinger, she smiled playfully, looking deeply into his pale blue eyes.

'Soon, my lover. But first, I have some news. We will be going on a little holiday to the United Kingdom. In the next few days.' He nodded. It was as they had both expected.

Then he took her in his arms, as they fell back onto the firm mattress. It would be over an hour before they had any further thoughts on their next mission. Through the open window, the traffic noise signalled the city awakening.

CHAPTER SIXTEEN

Bryan springs into action

As Bryan put the phone away in his back trouser pocket, he was already thinking through detail for the back story. In truth, he hadn't expected to have been contacted again, although it was a little flattering in a perverse way. Life in the old dog yet; after all, they still wanted him. They still thought he could do a job for them, which was more than Bunty seemed to think lately, anyway.

Bunty was already very accommodating of his little trips here and there, although the last one had been some time ago now. At the same time, she was rightfully never happy when left to run the place for long periods. After all, the post office did get busy on specific days – cashing cheques and drawing pensions, which affected a large number of the local inhabitants. No, he knew he would need to handle this carefully and provide a convincing backstory if he was to avoid any unnecessary stress.

‘Just had a text from Owain Smith. Remember him?’ he said, knowing full well she would not.

‘Never heard of him.’ Bunty looked up.

‘Old army pal. You must remember me mentioning him? Great fisherman. Has a place down in Ceredigion in mid-Wales. Runs a nice little carp lake. Says it is stacked full this time of year. Blighters are almost jumping out into the nets. Just waiting to be caught. Literally.’

‘Really.’ Bunty carried on reading her magazine. The escapades of Bryan and his friends always bored her and this was no exception. Besides, she was halfway through an article on cottage gardens, which had given her some ideas for the small, discarded patch of grass at the front of the shop. For the last few years, she had been constantly prodding Bryan to get something sorted, but there was always an excuse. After reading the article, she decided she would have to take matters into her own hands. There was even a small plan for him to follow.

‘Anyway, he has arranged for a few of us army pals to come down and fish there and stay in his wooden lodges. Night fishing is the best time,’ Bryan continued.

‘Really. When?’ Bunty had looked up, feeling her patience beginning to be stretched. Bryan was notorious for not getting to the point. He would go around the houses forever if she didn’t pull him up. ‘Spit it out, Bryan, for goodness sake!’

'Err well. It's a bit tricky really. Ideally leaving tonight…' His voice trailed off, under her steely gaze.

'Oh, Bryan. Bloody hell! You know I don't like being left here when it gets busy at this time of the week.'

'Only a few days. Hopefully,' he added, as an afterthought.

He turned around and exited pronto, as Bunty scowled after him. Scuttling up the stairs, he was soon in the small front bedroom as he grabbed an overnight bag and hastily filled it with a week's worth of casual clothing and underwear. Then he carried this through to the boot of his old Volvo estate, with an old sleeping bag and pillow that he hid underneath the muddy dog mat in the boot. As he was closing it and grabbing his wallet and phone, Bunty came out. From her expression, she was clearly still unhappy about the arrangement.

'So, you are literally leaving now?' She raised her eyebrows. Bryan flinched. It looked like she was on the warpath.

'Err yes. Best make good time. Quite a drive to deepest Wales after all. A good five hours at least.' He leant over and pecked her on the cheek.

'Haven't you forgotten something?' She glared at him.

'Err. What do you mean?' He looked around confused and into the back of the car. He saw the terrier looking wistfully out of the shop front door, head moving slightly from side to side. Bryan laughed as he walked over and stroked the animal by the scruff of the neck.

'Sorry, lad!' He walked over to place another kiss on Bunty's cheek.

'Fishing gear!' She fired the words at him like bullets, impossible to avoid, making him jump to attention.

Shit, what a fool! Bryan realised he had been away from this for far too long. He would have to up his game if he was to be of any use. He couldn't even stick to the story he had just invented.

'Oh yes, silly me.' He turned and trotted back into the cottage.

Five minutes later, he returned with one rod and reel and some assorted tackle. Just enough to convince a lay person that he might be able to catch something. Finally ready, he typed the address he had been sent into the satnav and waving goodbye, set off for a location in North West London.

***

The Turkish cafe that Bryan found himself sitting in was cheap and cheerful. More importantly, at this time in the late afternoon, it was relatively deserted, providing him with a perfect view of the terraced house from the window table he had secured on his arrival. A tired-looking young mum with two young children smiled over apologetically as the smaller child let out a shrill scream. Bryan flinched, inwardly giving thanks that Bunty and he had no children.

The large all-day English breakfast in front of him contained black pudding and fried bread, both of which were strictly forbidden for him to eat at home for health reasons. As he drank the thick, dark brown tea, Bryan reflected on his next plan of action. He had booked himself into a smart but simple bed and breakfast, handily placed near the corner of the street. Now he just had to wait for the light to fade a little, giving him the ideal excuse to enjoy an illicit meal. Importantly, he could see the car, familiar from his sighting back in Kent, parked on the road a door or two along from the address he had been sent on his burner mobile. There was only one problem. He seemed to have forgotten to bring the mobile. He had discovered this as he approached the outskirts of the capital, after frantically checking his jacket pockets and the overnight bag on the passenger seat, whilst trying to keep one eye on the road. Fortunately, he had remembered the address and had already inputted it into the satnav. No, the problem was that he may have left the phone back in Kent at the post office. Bryan had been tempted to turn around and go back for it, but he knew that may mean he failed to trace the woman in time. He just had to hope it didn't fall into the wrong hands, although thinking about it, Bryan realised it would mean nothing to Bunty.

Rush hour had started and there was far too much footfall for him to venture out now. Bryan needed a virtually deserted street for the next stage of the plan. He called over the owner, presumably Ali, after whom the eatery was named. The man, a slightly overweight Turk, beamed as he walked over.

'Everything okay, sir? The full English always fills the customers up. No complaints I hope?' His tired eyes smiled inquiringly at Bryan.

'No, not at all. Fine, lovely. Just wondered when rush hour dies down? I am waiting for a friend to arrive back.'

Ali nodded sagely. This area of London was full of flats and bedsits, many of which presumably had communal entrance halls and a myriad of doorbells outside. Bryan guessed half of Ali's customers were probably waiting for somebody to return home and let them in.

'Another half an hour. Once it starts getting dark. Then it is very quiet. This is a backstreet, remember, not a main road.' He gestured to the tea. 'Another? We give free top-ups.' He pointed to the menu on the wall: "Free hot drink top-ups" written in bright red pen. It was clearly their USP.

Bryan gulped it down and handed over the mug with a thumbs up.

Ali was right and once he had finished the second

mug of tea, the street lights had lit up and the number of pedestrians had reduced dramatically. Bryan decided the time for him to make his move was approaching. Thanking Ali, he left and crossed the road. There was little traffic. In fact, the house was a good hundred yards from the busy flow of traffic, which was just visible in the distance. Bryan walked further down to the quiet end of the street and then stopped and looked in an estate agent's window. Reading the details of the local properties for sale or rental was always a good cover when carrying out surveillance. A visitor to the area, taken in by either its ambience or convenience, and interested in the rental properties available would raise little suspicion.

Retracing his steps, Bryan wandered casually along the pavement until he reached the car. At that point, he dropped to the ground and made to tie his shoelace, whilst at the same time pressing the magnetic racking device to the underside of the car chassis, just beside the exhaust.

'Hey, what you doin''?'

Stopped in his tracks, Bryan looked up to see a large West Indian man with a thick-necked bull terrier on a lead.

'Oh, just tying my shoelace. Lovely dog.' Bryan leant forward and stroked the dog.

The man seemed surprised. Bryan had expected this – a little trick he used to put people at ease.

'Well, yes he is. This is Buster. Hey, you're not trying to take the car, are you?' The man was still doubtful. 'There's a car nicked around here almost every night,' he added.

Bryan shook his head.

'No, not at all. Actually, I'm just on the way to visit a friend.' He pointed to the front steps of the house number he had been given. 'I've got a terrier myself,' he added, looking down once again at the dog.

'Really. What type? Pit bull?' The man began to show interest. 'You got a pit bull, ain't yer? Good man!' The man opened his mouth as he laughed, showing several gleaming gold teeth. He moved to shake Bryan's hand and slapped his back.

'Err, no. Border terrier, actually.'

The man made a derogatory noise and turned away abruptly, whistling and laughing to himself. Once he had moved a good few yards away, Bryan took a last look to check the tracker was in position and then, after retying his shoelace, got to his feet.

Back in the bed and breakfast, Bryan continued to search for the burner phone he had used to contact Tim. Crucially, it had the tracker app on it. He checked through his bags and retraced his steps to the car outside. No sign of it anywhere.

Twenty minutes later and having still not located it, Bryan was faced with a dilemma. Should he return to get the phone, hopefully before it had fallen into the wrong hands? This would allow him to use the app on the burner. The other option, somewhat riskier but requiring less effort, was to get the app sent to his own smartphone and use that to monitor the car. He decided on the latter and downloaded the app using the access code he had been given.

CHAPTER SEVENTEEN

A crisis for Bunty

She stared blankly at the small item in her hand. A cheap-looking, little black pay-as-you-go mobile. Bunty had never seen it before. She had certainly never seen Bryan use it, but she recognised instantly that it was a burner. Why would Bryan be using a burner phone? She always used one when she contacted Dima, but Bryan? Bunty clicked the side button and the request appeared immediately for the password. She typed in her birthday. Correct first time. She was logged onto the phone. Oh dear, poor Bryan. She clicked on messages and saw one sent before Bryan had left for his fishing trip.

Woman turned up asking about the necklace. Renault Clio CT07 YLX

Bunty flicked through and saw that the reply had sent an address in London, presumably the registered address for the car supplied from the DVLA database. The bloody fool! So much for all that bollocks about going fishing. While she had been contacting Dima, Bryan must have followed the woman out of the shop and trailed her to get the car registration. Very clever, she had to admit. Suddenly, it dawned on her. If Bryan wasn't working for Dima, and she would know if he was, then he must be working for the British secret service.

As she poured herself a strong coffee, Bunty tried her best to compose herself, but the more she thought it over, the more she realised what she had done. She had alerted Dima, who would at this moment be planning some surveillance of the woman. The same woman that Bryan had raced off to shadow. More importantly, she had a crucial decision to make. Until now, she had not been aware of the registration number of the woman's car. Dima would no doubt have intended to use another method to track her down, perhaps via the internet. But now she knew the registration number, supplied courtesy of Bryan's sharp sightedness. The question was, did she pass this on to Dima? And if she did, would this place Bryan in imminent danger?

It should have been a difficult choice, but Bunty knew she had to remove Bryan from the equation. For that reason, she couldn't send the registration number on to Dima. She had to get Bryan out of harm's way first, and the simplest way to do that would be to enforce his return from London.

***

For the two hours after the app had been downloaded, nothing happened. It showed the car still parked in the street outside, a fact Bryan could verify by looking through the bedroom window. The street was deserted but well lit by the halogen street lights that seemed powerful enough to have illuminated a football pitch. It made Bryan yearn for the darkness of their little village. As he opened the fanlight window to get a little fresh air, the sound of the city drifted in, bringing car and music noise, which sharply contrasted with the wind and birdsong he heard back home.

In the rented room, he half watched a depressing documentary on food waste. He was just falling asleep as the credits began to roll, then the phone jerked to life. From the ringtone, Bryan knew it was an incoming call, rather than an alert from the app. He did not recognise the number.

'Hello?' he answered, rather tentatively.

'Mr Regis, Mr Bryan Regis.' An agitated female voice. He could detect a slight Australian drawl.

'Err yes, speaking. That's me.'

'It's your wife, sir. We are paramedics. We've just found your wife in her car, blocking a road near your house. It appears she has had some kind of blackout or attack. We haven't ruled out a TIA or minor stroke. The police have moved the car to a safe location and we have given her some adrenaline. She is back at home now. She is asking for you, sir. I'll just put her on for you.'

There was the sound of a phone being handed over. A new, familiar voice came on the line.

'Bryan, I am so sorry, darling. All this fuss…' The frail voice trailed off.

'Bunty! Are you okay, love?' After his initial shock, it was wonderful to hear her voice.

'Of course. Don't come back, Bryan. I'll be okay. I can always call them if it happens again. And I can call Jenny Alleyn; she is always here to support. Oh actually, I think she is away tonight…' Her voice trailed off.

'Don't be silly, love. I'll be back in an hour or so.'

'Really? I thought you had travelled miles?' Her voice was a little harder.

'Err, well a few hours. Don't worry, Bunty, I'll be back as soon as possible.'

He tried to reign in his irritation. Bunty's health had to take centre stage, but he did wish she would stop the questioning. Maybe she wasn't as ill as he thought.

He rubbed his stubble, now pushing through his weathered skin. He was now almost fully awake. A short stay to say the least. Checking out was fairly straightforward once he explained he had a family crisis and did not require a refund for the two unused nights he had booked.

***

Smiling to herself, Bunty repeated the process she had done before with this second burner phone. It had been a stretch, but she had pulled it off. Bryan was returning home. She had achieved her goal. Now she could contact Dima and pass on the information, safe in the knowledge that whatever happened, Bryan would not be a part of it. For her, however, she knew activities were far from over, but for now she had to prepare for Bryan's return. It was important that everything seemed just as he was expecting. Then she would wait for instructions from Dima.

CHAPTER EIGHTEEN

Dom gets a call

Dom awoke suddenly to the sound of his mobile phone vibrating. Jerking himself to life, he saw the time on the backlit screen was just after midnight. Bloody hell! He had only just got to sleep after a late meal; it always took him ages on a full stomach. He moved off the bed, creeping out of the room and into the study next door. Here, it was almost pitch black and the incessant low-pitched drone of their ageing gas meter gave enough ambient noise to block his conversation being overheard.

'Sorry, Dom, I know it's late!' He heard an anxious-sounding Tim at the end of the line. Dom sighed. Just the person he had dreaded would phone. A sinking feeling came over him once again. This was the last thing he needed.

'We need your help. A slight problem. The agent I told you about, our current agent, has an issue. Some domestic crisis back at base. Partner has come over unwell.' Tim rifled off the words. He doesn't want to give me a chance to say no, Dom thought to himself. 'Anyway, I need you to track the car of the woman I told you about, Penny Grainger. I've sent you a link to the tracking app you need to use. Just download it and you will see her car location. Our guy had already managed to put the transmitter onto the car before he got the phone call. We have reason to believe she can lead us to Dima and what he has planned, but she may be in danger. Remember the gun I gave you?' Almost breathless, Tim finally stopped talking.

'Of course,' Dom replied, keeping his voice lowered. How could he forget?

'Take it with you. You may well need it for protection,' he added. 'I have informed the police and they will send an armed response unit once we have your final location. And remember to use the direct voice record app I gave you to keep us abreast of any covert activity. The feed automatically dials into our boffins once it is activated.' Tim hung up abruptly, before Dom had a chance to put up any argument.

After the call had ended, Dom glided quietly around the bedroom and collected a full set of clothes, whilst Fay slept soundly. Remembering his previous experience several years ago, when he had spent a cold, sleepless night huddled in a front car seat, he also grabbed a high tog fleece, a woollen beanie hat and some gloves. After dressing in the toilet, he moved downstairs and wrote a note.

My cousin has phoned me. Partner admitted to hospital. Driving down to see them. Can you phone work and let them know I won't be in tomorrow? Speak soon. Love you. D x

Checking his watch, Dom crossed out "tomorrow" and replaced it with "today" and left the note on the kitchen table, where his partner would see it as soon as she entered the room.

He felt bad about lying but it had to be done. Once he had the car keys, Dom made his way to the shed and took the gun out from where he had hidden it under the beer-making equipment – purchased over a year ago in an attempt to kick start a new hobby. The collection of apparatus already lay discarded between the lawn mower and some open shelves holding a variety of power tools, and provided the perfect hiding place. Dom stared at the gun. He had carried one before, but his previous assignments had involved supporting the service by using his linguistic skills. This was another level.

Once he had left the house, Dom climbed into his old SUV. He normally cycled into work and the car was still showing some signs of its last recent outing, and he quickly disposed of a discarded energy drink can and several empty crisp packets strewn on the back seat.

The download had taken some time using the unreliable house wifi, but the tracking app was finally installed on his phone. Opening it, he saw it showed a map, similar to his own car's satnav. However, rather than displaying his own car's progress, the app was tracking the progress of the car driven by Penny Braithwaite. Simple, but effective. He pulled off the driveway and began his journey through the residential roads as he made his way out of the town's suburbs. The lights flickered on the roads as Dom sped towards the M25. The graphics flashed on the phone fixed in its cradle above the steering wheel, as the app updated itself every few seconds. In some ways, driving was easier at this time of night. There were no traffic jams and Dom had the roads more or less to himself, although there were still a number of vehicles with night-time deliveries.

Once he had reached the services on the orbital motorway, Dom pulled over for petrol, a packet of mints and a soft drink. How he could have murdered a cigarette now. He knew the act of chewing would help keep him awake and stave off the craving, but stopped himself after the third mint and checked the position of the car he was following on the tracking app. He could see it was now heading towards the South West on the M3. It seemed madness; what was he doing in the middle of the night? But it was too late now and bizarrely, he was caught up in the thrill of the chase. His life seemed to have more purpose than his role at the university. In fact, now he reflected on it, he was certain his actions now were more likely to have an impact on others' lives than any of his efforts with his students.

It was a further three and a half hours before the car he was following finally came to a halt up a side street in a small Cornish fishing port. Despite being well past midnight, the moon's reflection off the river estuary and the English Channel meant the town still seemed eerily awake, unable to sleep. The roads were all deserted, giving him a chance to get a full view of the location. He had driven past the target and pulled in on the opposite side of the road about fifty feet ahead. In the car's side-view mirror, Dom could just make out a slim woman ascending a flight of steep steps up the cliff. The name of the cottage was displayed on a piece of slate by the thick stone wall. He turned around in the driver's seat once she was out of view, and using his infrared telescopic lens, managed to focus on the writing: Seagull Cottage. Then he drove further up the hill and pulled over into a small layby, ignoring the angry "No parking – passing space" sign in front of him. At this time of night, he reasoned it was unlikely that a local vigilante group were checking for non-resident parking.

He picked up his phone and sent the details of his location to Tim. Then he reclined both front seats and pulled his sleeping bag over from the back seat. It would be an added bonus, but he may just get some sleep before dawn in an hour or so. He was parked in a quiet lane, with all the housing situated back down the hill in the direction of the village.

CHAPTER NINETEEN

Dima sets a trap

Dima thought carefully before coming to the decision. The last thing he wanted was to generate any unwanted attention when everything was going to plan. However, it was undeniable that Bunty's message had told him this woman had suspicions about the letter and the postcard. This alone was enough to spur him into action. He knew the words he had written off by heart. There was no mention of the codeword "necklace" in either of them. So how had she known about it? He racked his brain. Surely it couldn't have been just by chance. And then he remembered. It wasn't just communication by post; emails had also been sent. So it was clear that the woman had also seen these, presumably by accessing the email account of the dead TV presenter.

It took some time but he managed to locate the emails he had sent – they lay in the trash folder of the fake email account he had used and had not been fully deleted. One was cryptic, the other was not. However, the chances were, she couldn't have picked up on the word if she had not understood both emails. So the woman must have been able to access the emails on Stewart's computer and solved the cryptic crossword clues to decipher the instructions. It was doubly worrying. Dima was musing over this a little further when Shona appeared in the bedroom.

'Don't tell me you came all this way to see your beautiful girlfriend, only to spend all your time on that damn phone.' She was making a joke of it, but was still looking down at his hand in dismay.

Dima smiled. He had not reckoned on having to pay Shona quite so much attention. Once she had told him she had decided to close the shop for the duration of his stay, he had guessed that this constant companionship would be one of the unspoken consequences. Looking around the small room, he was beginning to feel decidedly trapped compared to his free-living bachelor lifestyle, meeting up with a range of different friends most nights, with no commitment beyond spending several hours in their company.

'Sorry!' He looked up smiling. 'How about a trip out somewhere nice? It's lovely weather. Some sightseeing maybe. Can you recommend anywhere?'

Shona looked a little disappointed. 'I thought we could stay in and talk about us. You know I want to come over and visit you in Russia. I wanted to check the best flights and what transfers I need.'

Dima smiled again. 'Of course, but let's go somewhere nice. We can have a meal out. How about Oxford?'

'Well, yes, I suppose. I hadn't thought about it, but now you mention it, it's only about half an hour.'

'Great. I want to see the artwork in the Ashmolean while I am over anyway. And then we can eat out. I'll book a table. I've heard Browns is a great place from friends who were over recently.'

These were both true. Dima smiled. He prided himself on remembering useful facts that he could have at hand when he needed to produce a cover story or develop a change of plans. Shona nodded enthusiastically. The more she thought about it, Oxford sounded like a great idea. The dreamy spires and green spaces, combined with the upmarket shops and restaurants were undeniably romantic. This could be the perfect setting to kickstart their relationship to the next stage, hopefully something more permanent.

There was another reason of course for Dima to choose the location. Once there, he would send the email from that same account he had not used since the last attack. It would be a perfect place to dispose of the burner phone, plus as an international location, it was probably second only to London in the south of England as a tourist destination. Monitoring of calls made from such a location would be much harder for the UK counter terrorism services. He had learnt that from the

Salisbury incident, where it had been all too easy to identify the agents' activity. Of course, they had left the country immediately, whereas Dima intended to stay on a little longer.

An hour later they were standing in one of several interconnecting galleries on the third floor of the world-famous museum. The cavernous rooms housed an expansive impressionist collection, with work from most of the modern masters. Absorbed, Dima spent a considerable time viewing each painting. In fact, it was beginning to stretch Shona's patience, although she had enjoyed seeing the Picasso paintings and a famous Rodin sculpture. Frustrated, she had walked ahead as he seemed to spend an eternity viewing each painting in turn, following the same routine: observing from a distance and then close up, followed by slowly reading all the information supplied in detail below each frame. In the end, Shona returned to try and speed him up, but of course he was nowhere to be seen, which was even more infuriating, as she was now stuck waiting for him in a place she wanted to leave.

***

Meanwhile, Dima had become aware of some unwelcome company. He had just spent a good ten minutes admiring a particularly fine example of pointillism, when he became aware of a presence at his shoulder. An older man in a heavy winter coat was staring directly at the painting. Nothing wrong there, Dima reflected, except that he was pretty sure this was the same man he had caught in the reflection of the glass entrance doors following behind them when they'd first entered the museum. The man was clearly sweating under the weight of the thick coat on such a warm day. This struck Dima as odd. Then there was the fact that the man had been standing behind him when viewing the last three paintings. And his hands were in his pockets and had been for the last ten minutes. Dima looked away whilst he considered his next move. This was too public a location to consider anything other than a swift attempt to lose his possible tail.

'Excuse me?' His thoughts were interrupted by a voice, with a slightly foreign intonation.

He turned to see the man moving towards him. Dima looked down and saw the silver blade glisten in the man's hand. He seized his chance and made for the lift he had seen earlier as he had climbed the stairs to this floor.

It was a small lift, with a sign stating it could take no more than six people. As he reached it, the door was closing with a family, including a young boy in a wheelchair, about to descend to the lower floors. He stretched for the door and managed to squeeze through the closing gap, to the alarm of the family. There was barely enough space as the door finally slid into the closed position. As he turned and looked back through the glass panel, Dima could see the man floundering as the heavy coat impeded his progress.

It took about half a minute for the lift to reach the lower ground floor, and Dima immediately turned left and strode towards the cafe, built into the foundations of the building. This was by far the busiest area of the whole museum and he was soon walking side by side with swarms of other visitors. There was no sign now of the man and Dima assumed he had given up the chase. To be sure, he turned off the main corridor, taking refuge in the men's toilets. This would be a good place to lie low for a while.

***

It was to Shona's relief that when Dima eventually did appear, rather sheepishly from the men's toilets on the lower ground floor, he suggested they head off immediately for a drink before their meal. In fact, she was taken aback as he took her arm and whisked her out through the main entrance. The narrow lanes were jammed with students and tourists. It appeared none of the people who passed them, using their phones as cameras and wearing branded sweatshirts and scarves from the university shops, were locals.

As they arrived at The Turf Tavern, Dima suggested she try to find a seat while he ordered the drinks. The old building was dimly lit, with few windows, meaning visibility inside was poor even when it was sunny outside. Once she was out of view, he pulled out his mobile and connected to the Gmail account. He had spent the night before finding the email address he had contacted to get the messages read out all those years ago. Then he had committed it to memory. In the email body, he typed the message:

Easy cash from discovery [10,4] 1900

He smiled. An easy clue for any seasoned cryptic crossword player. How ironic that solving it would necessitate her death. He would also send it to his agent; they would be there at seven p.m., waiting. If the woman did turn up, then like the TV presenter, she would know too much and have to be silenced for the sake of the ongoing operation. If she didn't appear, then for the moment at least, she would be spared. But past experiences had taught Dima that this was unlikely to be just a coincidence.

The bar staff had returned with his drinks and Dima weaved his way through the crowded public bar, almost unchanged for nearly five hundred years, to where Shona sat contentedly beside the door leading to the small, enclosed beer garden.

CHAPTER TWENTY

Bryan's return

All the lights were out when Bryan finally returned home. Good news, Bunty must be in bed asleep, rather than waiting up for him. Just to be sure, he had parked a little way back up the lane to avoid the noise of the car waking her. It was the early hours and he left his bags in the car, entering the house quietly through the back door. However, as soon as the key entered the lock, his faithful companion started barking, on guard duty. Bryan switched on the kitchen light and stepped out of his shoes, hanging his jacket on the peg on the back door and placing his car keys on the worktop. He patted the terrier and stroked his coat, as the dog lay down and rolled over, demanding some attention from its master.

Bryan was shattered and feeling his age. He vowed this would be his last manoeuvre; he would be volunteering his services no more. Creeping through the room, he turned right and slowly mounted the steep staircase. On the landing, he stopped as he prepared himself for the state his beloved Bunty was likely to be in.

Meanwhile, in the bedroom, a wide-awake Bunty had heard Bryan open the back door. She hid the burner phone she had been using to communicate with Dima under the mattress, deciding she would dispose of it when Bryan was out and about tomorrow. Quickly, she rubbed the pre-prepared mix of chilli and garlic powder under her lips and around the inside of her mouth. It took effect immediately and she began to sweat profusely. Breathing hard, Bunty cupped her hands under her nose. Foul, musty breath. The curtains were drawn, the room bathed in near darkness, just a crack of moonlight peering in around the window edge.

Outside the bedroom door, the noise of Bryan's steady tread could be heard as he mounted the stairs. Laying back, she threw around the duvet, attempting to make herself look as uncomfortable as possible, whilst she waited for the door to open. The transformation to a sick patient, bedbound for several hours, was complete.

CHAPTER TWENTY-ONE

Penny takes the bait

Dom was feeling particularly fed up. The few hours' sleep he had managed to get had been his most uncomfortable for years and now he could barely keep his eyes open. He would definitely have to book some accommodation if he needed to stay another night. He had already decided to ask at the pub later. Fortunately, he had enough bottled water to clean his teeth with the toothpaste and brush he had grabbed when he left earlier. Reassuringly, in the rear mirror, he could see the car he had followed was still parked at the foot of the steep steps.

An hour later and there was still no sign of the woman he had followed. Dom was now starving and decided to leave the surveillance in order to locate some hot food. Once he had walked down to the quayside, he spotted a small cafe on the other side of the bridge. Much as he would have been happy to eat in, he ordered fish and chips to take away, together with a can of coke and a coffee. On the way back, he passed the convenience store and despite the temptation of the cigarette packets behind the counter, he left with just two packets of chewing gum. As he walked back, Dom was relieved to see that the woman's car hadn't moved in the thirty minutes that had elapsed since he had vacated his post.

Soon, he had eaten the food and was drinking the coffee, with the can saved for an extra energy boost later. Still there was no movement. Dom had managed to grab a paper when he purchased the gum – not his usual trusted *Guardian*, but the only red top that was left in the store. Getting more and more frustrated with its coverage, he read the paper with one eye on the rear-view mirror. Then, unintentionally, he slept.

***

After arriving in the early hours of the morning, Penny had slept in once again. It was becoming a feature of her stay in the cottage. The fact that, unlike in London, there were no immediate neighbours to wake her up was probably the reason why she did not surface until mid-morning. That, and the absence of any building work, and just possibly the sea air.

After a shower, she attacked the fridge. Twenty minutes later, she was searching the bureau again to look for any further leads relating to Stewart's death.

There was nothing and she began to face the fact that her search had hit a dead end. As she started to pack her suitcase and return the keys to Trevelyan, a thought struck her. Maybe she had missed some more emails. She logged into Stewart's computer and accessed his email account. As it opened up, she stared at the screen. There was a new email from the same account that had sent the two previous emails all those years ago. It was not signed. No mention of Nikolai Johnson or the necklace this time. Just a simple message in the form of a cryptic crossword clue.

Easy cash from discovery [10,4] 1900

It was obvious 1900 referred to the time; she presumed it was seven p.m. today. Looking at the clue, she was none the wiser. However, she knew she had solved the other cryptic message in one of the other two emails. Penny opened the browser and in the search engine, typed "solving cryptic crossword clues". She selected a reliable-looking link and was presented with a list of possible methods of solving the crosswords.

She spotted that the use of "in" or "from" in front of a word suggested the use of some of the letters from the subsequent word. So that meant part of the clue used the letters in the word "discovery". In some cases, the clue represented a synonym – a word or words meaning the same thing. It still didn't help much. She guessed the answer, which was two words of ten and four letters, was most likely to be the destination to go to at seven p.m. It was clearly some sort of rendezvous. This may be her chance to identify who the killer of Stewart was. Perhaps she should inform the police. Penny looked at her watch; it was nearly six o'clock. Her only contact was DCI Jones, who was in London. Even if she contacted her, it would be impossible for her to get there at that time. Explaining the situation to anyone else was likely to take too long. Even as she thought it through in her mind, Penny realised it sounded too far-fetched.

A few minutes later, it struck her that if the email had been sent to the computer, it may well be that the sender knew of her location. Of course, she was wrong, but she did not know this. If it was the case, then maybe the answer lay on the map on the chimney breast. Looking at the clue, she spotted that the word "cove" was part of the word "discovery". Surely that worked as a cryptic clue. It said "from discovery" and the word "cove" had come from the word "discovery". This helped a lot because she now traced her finger along the coast, reading out the names of the different coves as she moved from east to west.

There weren't many listed on the map. Penny read off Parson's cove, laughing to herself as she visualised a Victorian clergyman in a full knitted bathing suit, relaxing in a deckchair, water just lapping at his toes. As she traced her finger across the estuary of the River Fowey, she saw the cove to the west of the main port: Readymoney Cove. What had the clue stated? Penny refreshed the laptop screen. The clue was "easy cash from discovery". "Easy cash" could be considered "ready money". She had solved it. Looking at her watch, she saw she was just in time. It was half six and the drive was about five miles.

CHAPTER TWENTY-TWO

Penny takes the bait

Dom was woken by the sound of a group of laughing teenage boys banging on the car roof. Little shits! How long had he slept for? He was out of the car and chasing them down the road before he realised the time on his watch was approaching six o'clock. He must have slept for the whole afternoon! He felt terrible. Worse than before, and that was saying something. The last time he had felt this bad it had been jet lag after attending a conference in Malaysia. Still, the car had not moved. He was even wishing he had brought the bloody marking with him, he was so bored, when just after half past six, he saw the woman quickly descend the steps and start up the car. He adjusted his rear-view mirror. As she drove past him up the hill, he counted to ten before following at an appropriate distance, keeping the car just in view as it weaved up the single-track road.

***

What Penny had not factored into her calculations was managing to get the car out of Looe via the narrow lane that led up the steep hill beyond the cottage. In the middle of summer, this route would be a non-starter due to the traffic generated by the myriad of caravan parks on the cliff top above. However, at this time of year, she had assumed it would be quicker than driving back into the town and taking the main road out to Liskeard, followed by the artery road towards Fowey. It certainly looked that way on the map. After she had reversed twice, once for a people mover filled to overflowing by a large family and then for an impatient fish delivery van, Penny realised ten minutes had already passed and she had made virtually no progress. The car had travelled about fifty yards up the hill. Welcome to Cornwall, she thought to herself. To make it worse, she had only realised after setting off that her phone registered less than twenty percent battery life. There was no time to turn back now. It would have to be enough.

However, the small car was soon hurtling along the cliffs, slowing down only to negotiate its passage through a few scattered villages, before speeding up again when the road widened and the lower hedges meant she could see oncoming traffic. The wind whistled by whilst she drove through the unsheltered farmland. As the light began to fade, Penny finally passed the sign welcoming her to Fowey and trundled into the town. At the top of the hill, with the harbour nestled either side of the still water below, she followed the brown tourist information sign for the cove and was directed to a small municipal car park. Virtually deserted, she parked under a street light, beside a couple of cars, presumably owned by locals. Beside the entrance was a footpath sign pointing to the beach and the small National Trust property St Catherine's Castle, which Penny could see was perched on the cliff above it.

Taking her mobile phone and a small torch she kept in her jacket pocket for when she put the bins out, Penny made her way down the winding footpath to the mouth of the cove below. The houses on the edge of the small modern housing estate had gardens that backed onto the narrow tarmac track, and Penny was reassured by the lights she could see in the overlooking windows. Would anyone come to her rescue if she needed help, she wondered.

Within a few minutes, Penny was standing on the small concrete promenade flanked by what appeared to be a collection of picturesque rental cottages on one side and a small kiosk on the other. All she could hear was the sea, lapping the edge of the beach. No noise was emitted from the accommodation, apparently vacant in low season. The kiosk, in the same concrete block as the toilets, was now closed with no sign of life, the doors locked with a large metal bar across them. The two benches beside looked out into the cove and were both unoccupied. A sign beside them warned of prosecution for unsociable outside drinking, presumably more of an issue in the long summer evenings.

Staring out into the English Channel in the last light before dusk turned to night, Penny marvelled at the natural beauty of the small cove, nestling below the steep cliff. Looking upwards, she saw the very small grey stone turret perched on the barren cliff edge. She could just make out the thin vertical arrow slits that had been built into the medieval stone walls. It looked like it belonged on the set of *The Lord of the Rings* and she imagined the characters from the film she had seen on television moving around in the shadows. Distracted, she reminded herself to check in the local tourist guide to find out if it had ever seen active service. It was narrow and just two storeys high.

As she looked, Penny noticed a small flash of light from within the tower. Was this where the rendezvous was taking place? Was this the signal, like a call to prayer, beckoning the accomplice to come up for the meeting? Feeling the adrenaline kick in, Penny wondered why she had come here. Her immediate thought was to turn around, get back into the safety of the car and drive back to the comfort of her own home. But she did not. This was her chance to see who was responsible for Stewart's death. She intended to get within earshot of the meeting and then record it whilst in hiding. She decided she could pass the recording on to the police later.

Walking across the promenade, Penny saw a small gate and a sign indicating a well-trodden path leading to the National Trust property. Once again, she was aware of the complete isolation. There was no sign of anybody else in the vicinity. Was the meeting already taking place inside the tower? As she stepped further forwards, Penny switched her mobile on and then opened the voice recorder app, hoping there was enough charge to record the conversation.

***

Shadowing her at a far enough interval to avoid being seen, Dom drove into the small car park a few minutes after Penny had arrived. He kept his distance as he watched the woman ahead of him walk up the narrow footpath that rose up the cliffs. Careful to stay out of sight from his vantage point a hundred yards behind her, Dom had also seen the light shine from the ruined castle. Immediately his training kicked in from several years back. The chances were, this was a trap. He saw now that the light was intended to lead Penny to be ambushed, rather than to signal to a waiting fellow conspirator. It was standard practice. Duty bound, Dom knew he had to follow her. For him there was no other option. Looking over his shoulder, he cursed as he saw no sign of the police support Tim had promised. His phone, which he had switched to mute, showed no messages, although it was unlikely he would pick up a signal in such a remote place. He regretted not sending a message earlier, whilst he still had a strong signal. Around him there was an eerie silence, broken only by the sea dragging itself slowly up the small beach, before combing back down again.

The woman's bright green jacket still stood out against the barren scrub and brush foliage on the hillside, as the sun began to set even further. Dom saw her take the left fork where the path split. From his own vantage point, some thirty yards behind, he could see the right fork was a winding track that led to a promontory, sticking out slightly above the ruined castle. Once Penny was out of sight, he moved quickly to take the right fork and then broke into a run, almost tripping on one occasion where the roots of a tree had made a hook across the surface of the path. Cursing under his breath, he stopped and listened as he rubbed some life back into the sore ankle. There was still no sound. Breathing a quick sigh of relief, he realised that nobody had heard him stumble.

Less than a minute later, he was in a position where he could clearly see a figure moving stealthily around within the weather-beaten stone walls. Groping around with his right hand, Dom felt the cold metal of the hand gun he had in the inner pocket of his jacket. It was hardly reassuring. Please God, he didn't have to use it. After all, he saw his role as intelligence gathering – that was what matched his profile. He was an academic for Christ's sake! He had been totally useless on the shooting range during his recruitment training, leading to the eponymous nickname Dead-eye Dom based on his failure rate. Every day his inaccuracy had increased, much to the amusement of his fellow trainees. No, Dom had the gun purely as a last resort, for protection if he was cornered. Panic began to set in. He felt sure it would not be a good outcome if it relied on his discharging the firearm.

As he looked again, Dom saw the light, flashing on once more in the small castellated tower. He had to admit it was a clever place to lure an unsuspecting victim. It was highly likely the person in the tower was an accomplished marksperson. He knew from Tim that the woman, who he remembered was called Penny Grainger, was a literary agent who had accidentally stumbled over the Necklace spy ring; it was hardly likely she would be able to hold her own in a shoot-out. His only hope was to cause a distraction, allowing her to make an escape. So, why not advise her now? Of course, the reason was obvious: his presence there was primarily for surveillance, to establish who they were dealing with and report back to Tim, who would in turn report back to his superiors.

Listening, Dom realised the seagulls were no longer circling above, their calls having stopped some time ago. Instead, he could occasionally see the flashing images of bats moving around in the thin line of trees above him. The waves were crashing in more loudly on the shore and he could see a single light flicking out at sea, most likely a lone fisherman making the most of the still sea, dropping or picking up a lobster pot. Of course, it could be a support vessel sent by Tim, but this seemed unlikely.

He removed the high-power lens Tim had issued him with from its small cylindrical case, which he had been carrying in his other inner pocket. Switching it on, he manipulated the zoom. When he selected the infrared facility, the image came into clear focus and Dom could see that the person held not just the torch in one hand, but a gun behind their back in the other, carefully hidden from the view of the approaching woman. Looking to the path below, Dom could make out Penny's head in clearer detail as she approached the ruin, the torchlight catching her beautifully symmetrical features framed by her black dreadlocks. As he watched, Dom realised she appeared to be completely unaware of the ambush that awaited her. He would have to find a way to alert her to the impending danger before it was too late.

CHAPTER TWENTY-THREE

Executing the plan

Bryan was fully absorbed in checking the latest order from their wholesaler when the text came through to Bunty's burner phone. Fortunately, he seemed to have accepted both her sudden illness and subsequent equally sudden recovery. As she looked, Bunty saw the familiar cryptic clue giving her the next instruction.

After checking personal German banknotes [3,3]

In some ways, she found this charade somewhat tiresome and, bearing in mind the amount of electronic communications that flew around the world each second, also rather unnecessary. But Dima was adamant. It had been a failsafe system he had used with great success for previous attacks. Reluctantly, she attempted to decipher the instruction. Thinking hard, it took her some time to work out the answer. German banknotes were Deutsche Marks and therefore she supposed "personal" meant "your marks", so checking them could mean "on your marks", which was of course followed by “get set”. So now the plan was in motion. Bunty knew the next stage was to link up with the other agent involved in the attack. This involved driving around the M25 and to South Essex, a journey of just over an hour. The excuse had been prepared in advance; she had been expecting this moment. The outfit had been already created.

‘That training I need to do?’ She called out into the shop, where Bryan was standing once more beside his beloved cheese display with a customer who had just arrived. He looked up, slightly agitated that he might lose a sale.

‘No problem, love. I won’t be a sec. I’m just advising this gentleman,’ he replied abruptly. ‘Now, sir, can I recommend the Kentish Brie?’ he continued.

Great, by the time he has realised I am off he won’t be able to start any form of interrogation, Bunty thought. Quickly, she returned over to the wholesaler and signed off the order as he returned from depositing the last of it in the back of their open garage, which served as the overflow storeroom. Then, head down, she entered through the back door and made her way upstairs to collect the case she had packed in anticipation a few days ago.

Less than a quarter of an hour later, Bunty had returned downstairs with the suitcase fully packed and placed it behind the counter as she entered the shop. Bryan turned as she entered.

'Bloody hopeless. Fussy eater. Total waste of time. He went through the additives and E numbers on every bloody piece of cheese we sell. Took me ages to read them all out, of course. Then said he'd leave it.'

'I'm leaving, Bryan.'

'Eh, what?' He stopped mid-rant.

'That training course for the post office. You know, for the new system they keep promising? They've sent me a message. They've got a space. I can go earlier. Only the other day you were moaning about how much quicker it will be once we get it installed. This would speed up the process, Bryan,' she lied fluently.

'Great.' Bryan nodded, sagely. 'Makes sense. That's good news.'

'Yes, the only trouble is, it's in Essex. Billericay to be precise.'

'Bloody hell!' Bryan's cheeks flushed. 'Where's bloody Billericay? Essex, you say? That'll be a nightmare each day over the Dartford bridge and tunnel. And there's the charge as well.' Bunty could sense he was getting more agitated.

'Calm down, Bryan,' she replied. 'I'm staying over. It's only one night. I'm going now and I'll be staying tonight and back late tomorrow evening.'

'Ah, one night. Well we could close the shop and I could come with you? A plus one, so to speak.' Bryan smiled as he used the term. 'Yes, I've always fancied a trip over to rural Essex.'

‘No, Bryan. It’s hardly rural. Looks like it’s based on a business park on the outskirts of the town. It’s just a standard training course. Sandwiches for lunch and lasts all day. Then I’ll drive straight back. And I won’t get there until later this evening so I’m taking a piece of that quiche and some salad that I’ll eat in the hotel room,’ she added.

Bryan pulled a face at the prospect of such a meal. He would rather have had a good steak in a nice restaurant. Maybe it was better for Bunty to go to Essex on her own. Actually, now he thought about it, tonight was fish and chips night in their local and it was always a good-sized portion, unlike so many places these days. The cricket team would be in as well, so there would be some others he could chat to if the landlord was busy serving. No, much better to stay and have an evening in the village. Besides, he hated the drive at this time of day – wall-to-wall traffic jams when he could be walking the dog.

‘Okay. I’ll manage things this end,’ he replied, nodding, his mind made up.

***

Jesse had been careful not to jolt the small tender in any way whilst he drove the motorcycle back, despite the regularly appearing potholes, especially on the back roads he had used. Fortunately, the natural gyroscopic tendencies, together with a virtually traffic-free drive, meant when he finally dismounted and looked inside the pannier, he would have been surprised if there had been any spillage. After all, this stuff was grade one toxic, as he kept reminding himself. He kept the cycle helmet and gloves on just in case and parked well out of view of the rest of the campsite, behind his bin and washing line. Still, one couldn't be too careful and he kept checking for any figures advancing to his far corner of the park. He had already purchased a large metal bowl, and using tongs, he removed the box holding the tender with the skill of a surgeon and placed it in the centre of the bowl; it could have been an appendix.

Next, he held the tender firmly in the tongs with one hand, while he held a long, thin screwdriver in the other. Turning the tender over, he saw three small screws in a line. Carefully, he attempted to turn the first screw. No luck. They had obviously been tightened as much as possible to avoid the casual undoing in customs, obviously banking on the fact that getting a power screwdriver would be too much effort, although he thought this type of tool was probably the mainstay of most customs and excise rummage crews.

Jesse was not surprised, but it was frustrating as the noise of the power tool would be likely to attract unwelcome attention – something he had been at pains to avoid. It also added an extra element of risk, although he had a clamp to ensure the tender stayed firmly stationary. Fortunately, he had already put the drill on charge, and once he had selected the correct driver head, he found all three screws came out easily. At this point, he now realised he must be extremely careful not to pierce the container. Just a drop of the chemical weapon could wipe out most of the immediate neighbourhood. Using two pairs of tongs, he successfully removed the top of the tender casing, including the mock coal stockpile, revealing the spherical clear plastic container that held the liquid. Carefully, he removed the tube and placed it in a small metal safe – an approximate cube with sides of about three inches – which he had purchased a few days earlier. Then he locked the safe, using the combination he had already set, and placed it by the hedge at the back of his plot under some tarpaulin.

Beside him was a washing bowl he had already prepared with a mild bleach solution. He washed his hands and arms up to the elbow in it, then dried them and rubbed an anti-oil gel over his hands, trying to cover inside all the small folds of skin. He removed all his clothes, other than his underpants, leaving them in a pile to burn later. Then he had a very hot shower for five minutes, before shaving his face and head with a disposable razor.

Once he was dressed again, he could relax, and reaching across the cramped kitchenette, Jesse made himself an instant coffee. Now he had the chemical weapon securely stored and ready for when he needed it, he hoped the rest of the execution of the plan would be relatively easy. The package he had picked up several days earlier from the windmill's letterbox had given him full details of all the purchases he had needed to make and instructions regarding executing the plan. Jesse smiled to himself. That had been a stroke of genius on Dima's part, using a deserted property, presumably purchased as a part of an investment portfolio. A new letterbox had been installed, no doubt by unaware local builders on Dima's instructions, solely for this one delivery.

Looking at his phone, he saw that he had been sent two messages while he had been riding back from the handover. He opened the first. As usual, it was in the form of a cryptic clue.

Building for lower classes only [5,2,7]

It was quite easy to work out that the answer was the House of Commons, bearing in mind the advice he had been given on gaining the security officer role. The second message also contained a cryptic crossword clue.

Frozen in because? [3,5]

This was a much harder proposition. He finished the rest of the coffee, using it to wash down half a packet of custard cream biscuits. He would need to think more on this.

He took a five-kilometre run across the flat

marshland to clear his head. It was featureless and fairly desolate but was ideal for running, and he knew he needed to maintain his fitness levels. Once he was back, he collapsed on the narrow sofa. Although he had a slight frame, the cushions made of cheap foam with a thin covering of material sagged dramatically under him. It was when he was pouring himself a Diet Coke, cold from the fridge, that the answer came to him. Very clever. Now he just needed to know where and who the target was. He was still unaware of the answers to these questions, but he knew he would be told this soon. As he looked around at his grim surroundings, he reminded himself of the large deposit that had appeared in his off-shore bank account at the start of this week. The same amount would be deposited after the job was done. Financially, it would be well worth the effort.

Suddenly, he noticed two teenage boys cycling around the outside of the caravan on their mountain bikes. Pulling back the curtain, Jesse saw they had stopped just a few feet from where he had hidden the canister. Worried, he stood back in the lounge and positioned a mirror so he had a clear view, without being seen. The boys were now cycling in tightly decreasing circles until, inevitably, one of them fell off. As his bike flew forwards, the boy fell back, banging his head on the box. Before Jesse could do anything, the boy was standing up and kicking the metal box violently, until his friend cycled off, when, after one last glare at the offending item, he picked up his bike and also cycled off. A minute later, Jesse put his spare motorcycle gloves on and came out to check the safe box. It appeared that it was fully intact; there was no visible seepage. After weighing up the options, he placed it underneath the caravan, surrounded by a few bricks.

Inside the caravan, Jesse took out the ice cube moulds; he had purchased three moulds. He was over-compensating, he knew he was, but once he started the process, he didn't want to have to stop midway. Clearing the worktop, he laid out each mould. He had already checked that all three moulds would fit flat in the small industrial freezing unit he had purchased from a hospital supplies specialist in Birmingham, which was plugged into the mains and in the corner of the kitchenette.

It was later that day when he started the process. Reaching down into the holdall he had on the small table, Jesse took out the gloves he had purchased a week ago online from a laboratory supplier using a forged and untraceable credit card. He was ready now to start the process. Having checked there was still nobody outside the caravan, Jesse stepped outside and retrieved the metal box as quickly as possible, whilst following all the safety guidelines he had been given. It was just as he was climbing the two steps back into the kitchenette, treasure in hand, when he was stopped in his tracks.

'Time for a cuppa?' He recognised the voice

immediately and looked at his watch before replying.

'Yes, I think so.' He tried not to let his anxiety show as he spoke.

Bunty followed him in, locking the door behind her, before she sat down on the sofa, squeezing her legs under the pull-out table. The curtains were all drawn. The overhead light was on, together with a large halogen light, which placed the trays and kitchen work surface under the spotlight.

'So how far have you got? I came over as fast as I could.' She looked at the trays laid out. 'Just about to make it then?' Jesse nodded. He placed the safe on the table and unlocked it. Bunty stared into the small aperture.

'Careful. One drop will wipe out both of us.' Jesse spoke calmly, trying not to show alarm in his voice.

Bunty stood up and took several paces backwards into the small hall, allowing Jesse space to move the vial. He lifted it with extreme care, ensuring it knocked against nothing – one crack in the metal would be fatal. When it was safely standing on the worktop, he breathed a sigh of relief. Stage one completed.

He remembered the instructions he had been given by Dima and filled each of the ice cube holders two thirds full of distilled water, purchased from a local garage. Before he did this, Jesse heated the water in a kettle.

'Hot water, surely you want cold?' Bunty stared at

him.

'Little trick,' he replied. 'Hot water actually freezes quicker. Something to do with the bonds. I read it up on the internet when I researched this.' He was pleased to speak with a degree of authority on the subject. 'Normally, they would take three to four hours to freeze, but with the hot water and the top of the range freezer I purchased, it should be ready in under two hours.'

'Clever you.' She was impressed.

Slowly, he unscrewed the lid of the canister. Bunty held her breath. She had considered unlocking the door to allow ventilation, but it was too late now. She knew there would be no escape for her if this went wrong. She imagined the police arriving at the scene and wondered what they would make of finding two apparently unrelated bodies sprawled on the caravan floor. After a few seconds, the lid was off and Jesse had the pipette in his right hand, whilst the left hand was firmly clamped onto the vial, keeping it vertical. It was vital there was no movement of the canister. The pipette held enough for three drops. He also held his breath when he dropped the first into a hole in the plastic ice-cube holder.

Five minutes later, the trays were in the freezer and Jesse was placing the canister back under the caravan, throwing the gloves beside it. After a shower, he was sharing a cup of tea with Bunty at the table. As they finished their conversation, Bunty summarised the key points.

'So, you will bring the ice into the staff room, inside cool boxes with plastic ice blocks to keep it frozen?'

'Correct.'

'Then you will transfer this into the customised freezer storage area that you have created in a disused locker?'

'Correct.' Jesse nodded. 'You will be working as a waitress at the House of Commons. Have you sorted that yet?'

'No problem. Don't worry about that,' said Bunty, confidently. 'In all, I only need to be active for under ten minutes. I have checked and it is a contracted catering company. I've made an application to work for them under a false name. I just need to turn up, with a matching ID, which I have here.' She patted the pocket on the front of her waxed jacket. 'I have a copy of the uniform so I can just merge in with the waitressing team. If anyone asks, I'll say I was called in at the last minute. If they check, which I'm sure they won't, my details and photo will be on their staff database. And besides, I'll be out of there before they can check fully, so not a problem.'

'Makes sense. Once I see you approaching the security gate, I will walk and overtake you. Follow me into the staff room. Make sure you are carrying a large bowl that can hold ice cubes, so either bring fruit or something similar that we can quickly dispose of. The last thing we want to do is clean the bowl out before we add the ice cubes to it.'

'Agreed. And then I will make my way into the room they are eating in. I'll need to go in there once beforehand so I know the location.'

'Yes. When you get there, make sure the ice cubes get put into the drinks as soon as possible. We don't want them to melt or the solution will just be thrown away and wasted,' Jesse added.

At that moment, both their phones vibrated in unison. The last part of the puzzle had come through. Dima had used their group messaging system now.

Nice tab, for drinks [7]

They both looked at each other.

'Search me?' Bunty said, as she stared at the phone.

'Well, we've only got just over an hour to solve it,' Jesse replied. 'So we'd better give it some consideration.'

Ten minutes later and Jesse was alone again. The next stage was to ensure they stayed frozen on the way in. This was simple. He had placed more plastic ice packs, frozen overnight, into the pannier, which he had lined with insulating material. Checking his watch again, Jesse started to get ready to leave. It was as he was changing that the answer came to him. Very clever. It was certainly an audacious plan. Now he knew the target, the planning was complete. They just needed to execute it.

***

Bunty changed into her uniform in the service station toilets. She had sourced the fabric from one of the thousands of internet sites based in South East Asia, which were almost untraceable, and produced the outfit herself, matching the one she had seen on the promotional material for the catering firm. Back in the car, she checked her burner phone for further instructions. The message was brief, but its meaning was clear.

Tarts rearranged to sail a new course [5,6]

Not one of Dima's best, at best a clumsy clue, but it took Bunty less than a minute to work out that the first word was "start" by rearranging the letters. "Sail a new course" was to take a new tack, therefore the message was simple: start attack. Immediately, Bunty placed the fake security parking pass on the dashboard and drove off towards the House of Commons.

PART FOUR

TARGETS

CHAPTER TWENTY-FOUR

Ambush

As soon as she took the step forward, Penny regretted it. As a twig snapped, letting out a tight, brittle sound, the torch light spun round. It was like a searchlight and although the path was shrouded by overhanging branches, she felt sure she was now clearly highlighted in the beam. Instinctively, her body froze. Penny was less than thirty feet from the light source. Annoyed with herself, she wished she had chosen more inconspicuous clothing, rather than the almost luminous green jacket.

'Hello. Is that you?' The male voice sounded vaguely familiar, but she couldn't quite place it. Confident, but not overly loud.

Penny stopped. Instead of taking another step, she stood there rigid. Was this man really waiting for an accomplice after all? Suddenly, it dawned on her. Surely he would have called the person by name if he knew who he was meeting. No, she was sure now that this was a trap. He had been waiting for her and she had obliged. Stupidly, she had walked straight into the trap. Rather than her listening in covertly, instead it was Penny who had been ambushed herself. Bluff was her only chance. She switched on the recorder and walked forward.

The torch now illuminated the path in front of her. It moved with her, so she was now in its centre, and for a few seconds she could see the hooded man in front of her more clearly. He was standing at the end of the cliff, looking down at her as he stepped out from the entrance to the tower. There was something about his movement that looked familiar. Penny racked her brain. He was still in the shadows. Then the figure moved further forward, dragging the leg more noticeably. Close enough for her to fully recognise him.

'Mike?' Penny was confused. 'What are you doing here?'

'I couldn't believe you'd turn up.' He laughed as he continued. 'After all, you are a media agent, not a secret agent, aren't you? You should have stuck to what you're best at!' He waved the gun in front of him to make sure she could see it. 'Now I am going to have to kill you. What a waste.' He shook his head as he laughed once more.

'I don't understand. You mean it was you who killed Stewart?' Penny was still dazed from the discovery.

'Haven't you worked it out yet?' He looked smug, giving a self-satisfied smile. 'That stupid fool you represent had to be silenced. We gave him a chance, but he couldn't keep his mouth shut.'

'Why?' She couldn't understand; it was beyond comprehension. 'Why did Stewart have to be killed? It doesn't make sense. He was just a retired TV presenter. He wasn't a threat to anyone.'

'He didn't know a lot. But what he did know was too much.' Mike was even more confident now. After all, he had the gun.

Penny thought hard. Did she want to let Mike know what she had discovered about Nikolai Johnson and the necklace? The answer was, probably not. But she had to think of some way of putting him on the back foot. Instead, she decided to try a different tactic.

'The police are following right behind me,' she lied.

'Perhaps they are, but I will be long gone.' He paused. 'And I am not so sure they are anyway. If you had told them, they would have come themselves. They certainly wouldn't let you come this close unaccompanied and I can't see any sign of them here.' With that, he swung the torch slowly in a full circle. 'So, you worked out our little riddle?' he continued, changing the subject.

'Readymoney Cove. Easy really,' Penny replied. It seemed pointless now to believe she had been pleased to have worked out the clue.

'Easy, but I am afraid it has sealed your fate. Just like the man you represented. All those years that

Stewart passed on messages for us completely oblivious to what he was doing. I assume you found the messages. You must have done, to have started digging around.'

'Letters and emails, yes. Mentioning the necklace and from Nikolai Johnson.'

'Oh yes.' He laughed. 'Nikolai Johnson. And you heard about the necklace. I am afraid now that you know too much.'

'Tell me why Stewart had to die,' Penny said bravely.

'Well. I can't see it matters now. He was broadcasting messages for us, as I said, completely unknowingly. We had another operation in the planning stages. If he mentioned anything at all then it could have been blown. As it is, the execution of it is now well underway. So we had to test him, hence the fake interview. It was so easy for me to invent the company and then say we were producing a computer game. You would be amazed how short of stories these channels are. They lapped it up. I put the money in his account upfront and that lured him to the interview. He was almost home and dry, when he mentioned the fan mail messages on letters and postcards; that was his input. That was his mistake, saying he had control over the messages. We had to silence him.'

'I don't understand. On the CCTV I saw you exit five minutes before Stewart left the building.'

'Once I had left, I changed into a black hoodie and tracksuit bottoms. I shot back on the scooter I had hidden behind the bins away from the CCTV cameras,' Mike continued.

'But how did you ensure you left before him?'

'Easy.' He seemed pleased at his ingenuity. 'I moved his case and spoke to him as we left so he forgot it. Then when he realised it was missing, he had to go back.'

'I was right. I knew it was an assassination.' The realisation hit Penny.

'Yes. And now you.' Aiming his gun at Penny's face, Mike took a step forward. She could see his features now. How different, she thought, from the mild-mannered man she had chatted to only a few days ago in that suburban kitchen. She felt sick. There seemed no visible means of escape.

A shot rang out, echoing around the bay. Mike moved slightly and turned around to see where it had come from. In that split second, Penny ran forward and with all her strength, launched herself at his unprotected torso. Taken unawares, he faltered and stumbled backwards, towards the cliff edge, a matter of feet away. Losing his balance, Mike began to fall down, dragging Penny over the side with him. She gasped, regretting being so foolhardy in following him to this remote location. Was this how her life was to end, falling to her death at a remote cove, clinging to a stranger as she played out some bizarre attempt at being a private detective? As she continued to be dragged, Penny felt her life flashing before her. What would her partner feel when they contacted him about her death? What had she really achieved in this life?

Suddenly, she felt another force. Her body was being pulled back away from the abyss. Looking behind her, Penny could see a man with an unruly mop of brown curly hair holding her ankles. Mike was now pulling ferociously at her jacket as he searched frantically for a better grip. In an instant, she loosened her arms from the inner lining and the coat slid over her shoulders and over the cliff, still in his grasp. At the same time, Penny was thrown backwards towards the man, as he quickly moved to one side.

They heard the loud scratching as Mike desperately scrambled, arms flailing wildly, trying to hold on to the damp undergrowth that fringed the cliff edge. Suddenly, it stopped. Then there was a sharp panic-ridden scream, rather like a wild animal caught in a trap, followed by a single thud as the body landed on the smooth wet sand below.

'Thank God you're okay.' Dom looked at her, relieved. He could hardly believe that between them, they had managed to avoid her being shot, probably killed. It had been point-blank range. He was secretly impressed that he had been able to move fast enough; ditching the cigarettes had clearly improved his fitness levels. Slowly, Penny rose to her feet and moved, rather unsteadily and still clearly in shock, to look over the edge. There was nothing, just a dark emptiness, with the sound of the sea lapping on the beach, now partially lit by the advancing moonlight.

CHAPTER TWENTY-FIVE

Nikolai Johnson unmasked

'Thanks. Penny.' She held out her hand as she introduced herself.

'Dom. Dom Stephens.' As he shook it, he smiled under his tousled hair. 'Long story. British secret service, Counter Surveillance division. We've been shadowing his spymaster, called Dima. It's a long story.'

'So you've been following me?' Penny looked shocked.

'To get to him, yes.' Dom frowned. 'Apologies.' Suddenly, he realised just how bad this sounded.

They both stood motionless. It was as if the shock had suddenly caught up with them. The sky was now dark and the air had turned to a cold freshness that only seems to occur at the coast.

As they turned and walked down the path, Dom explained the threat of an imminent attack.

Five minutes later, they were both beside the body on

the deserted beach. Penny's torch illuminated the velvet sand, smoothed clean by the evening's high tide. Sprawled unnaturally with both arms thrust outwards, there was no sign of life.

'So he was your client's assassin?' Dom quickly corrected himself. 'Sorry, your friend's assassin?' he said, pointing to the body. Penny nodded.

'And who was Nikolai Johnson?' she asked in turn.

'Well, that was the name used by the spymaster. He used the false name when planning the attack last time. That's why you found it on the emails and messages sent in to Stewart. Clever. Very clever. His agents knew the message was from him when they heard that name. In essence, he used it as a codename to trigger the attack.'

Penny stood still, her head spinning as she slowly put all the pieces together. Disappointed, Dom paced up and down. In his mind he had hoped, and indeed planned, to have extracted some details about the forthcoming attack from the man. Now he was dead, this seemed impossible. Once again, like the exchange at the railway exhibition, he appeared to have failed. Having one last thought, Dom knelt down and felt inside the black hoodie.

'Bingo!' He pulled out a small black mobile phone.

Fortunately, it was unlocked, and he could see that the man had been in contact with NJ – Nikolai Johnson, of course. There had also been several text messages. However, this all related to following Penny. He also checked WhatsApp and immediately opened the group named Necklace. The group had four members: NJ, J, M and B. Hadn't Penny called the man Mike? This matched with the conversation, which showed the user of the phone was listed as M. The identities of J and B were still a mystery to him. As he swiped back through the conversation, Dom stopped at one section in particular.

NJ: Is the attack ready?

J: Yes.

NJ: Good. Make sure you keep it secure and always frozen.

J: No problems. I have managed to get onto the security staff based at the Cabinet Office. Will swap when taken in.

NJ: Good. Make sure you call SM away before she has a chance to have any of it.

J: Will do.

Penny stared at Dom. His youthful features appeared to age in the short time he had been reading the messages. He gestured to her that he needed to make a call and took out his mobile, ringing Tim's number.

It took a while for Tim to answer. When he did, Dom sensed he sounded distracted, if not a little surprised. 'Hi, Dom. Any update?'

'The assassin is dead – a fall. I have managed to get some details of the attack.' He relayed the message to Tim.

‘Good God.’ Tim was quiet for a moment as he appeared to take onboard this information. Clearly, he had not been expecting to be given this information, or at least not by Dom. ‘So it is a planned attack on the Cabinet at the House of Commons?’ he continued.

‘Pretty much.’

‘Okay. Leave it with me. Come back to London, meet me there as soon as you can and keep in touch. You may still be needed. After all, we still don’t know the time of the attack or what form it will take.’ Tim rang off.

Dom stared ahead. Suddenly the weight of the responsibility hung heavily on his shoulders. This was it; he had to help stop an attack, an attack of national importance.

Penny stood silently away from him, lost in her own thoughts, still trying to come to terms with what had happened. How could Stewart’s death have been linked to a spy ring and an attack on the country? It was beyond belief. And now there was another death. She looked forlornly down again at the body beside them. It was only a few days earlier that she had been chatting to Mike. At the time, it hadn’t felt right; it wasn’t just that she had taken a dislike to his shrugged shoulders and dismissive attitude. It all fell into place now. The money paid up front had been by Mike to lure Stewart into the interview. He had placed the briefcase behind his chair, giving him time to leave and then return, changed, to kill Stewart, only to then race away on an unmarked scooter, avoiding CCTV. Penny thought hard. Did she believe Mike that it was a test for Stewart and he had failed by spilling the beans on the use of fans' messages sent to him, unscripted? Or had they planned to kill Stewart anyway? Now Mike was dead, she may never know.

The sound of the harsh acceleration of a car along the road that bordered the cove filled the air. Dom pulled himself out of his thoughts and summoned the energy to walk back to the car park. After all, this was no longer a time for thinking; this was a time for action.

Penny's phone sounded to register an incoming email. She stared at it in disbelief.

'What is it?'

'An email from the Nikolai Johnson account. I linked it to my email app on my phone just in case.' She held the screen up so Dom could see the message.

One less this time for tea with scout [3,6]

He shook his head. 'Means nothing to me, I'm afraid.'

CHAPTER TWENTY-SIX

Stopping the attack

Dom realised there was little that could be done in Cornwall after he had finished the phone call. Although Penny wanted to inform the police and wait with the body, he had convinced her it would be better to leave it for some unfortunate jogger or dog walker to discover. The death had all the hallmarks of an accidental fall from the cliff, where the path ran close to the edge. The body was still in its landing place vertically below. However, Penny had still argued, and reluctantly, he agreed to stop off and make an anonymous phone call to the police from the payphone on a garage forecourt he had seen when driving down earlier.

And so, after leaving Penny at the car park to drive back to pick up her belongings, Dom put his foot down and drove flat out towards Central London. It would normally take four over hours; somehow, he managed it in three and a half, clinging to the central barrier in the fast lane. He was low on petrol but knew he didn't have time for refuelling. He checked his watch; it was now just after eight in the morning and he realised he had been awake for over a day, with the exception of a brief few hours in the car's front seat. It didn't seem to matter, as the adrenalin fired him on. No time for a comfort stop, he crossed and recrossed his legs, trying to take his mind off his full bladder. The worn tarmac rolled past as the rain began to pelt down just before Andover, so heavy that the wipers struggled to keep his vision clear as they scrambled across the windscreen.

As he approached the capital, the deluge abated as quickly as it had started. Dom drove straight past the swarms of tourists, heading to the trade entrance at the back of the House of Commons, where he gave the security details he had only used once before, several years ago. After what seemed like an eternity checking them, the security official slowly shook his head.

'Sorry. This is not full clearance. You'll need to reverse up and exit, sir. This area is for high-level clearance staff only.' He waved his hand dismissively, to indicate Dom needed to turn around and drive back along the route he had taken into the compound.

'Look!' Dom said impatiently. 'I have been called to attend by Special Forces division by Commander Tim Coutts. It's a matter of the utmost importance.'

This had the effect of making the official look even more exasperated, but he shrugged his shoulders and turned, walking slowly over to the small grey portacabin located beside the entrance barrier. Through the tinted glass, Dom could just make out him having a heated discussion, presumably with his superior. After some consultation, the other person could be seen talking into a landline phone.

A few minutes later, a very stressed-looking Tim appeared from a doorway in the corner of the yard and marched over to Dom's car, angrily gesturing to the same security officer that the barrier should be raised immediately as he did so. Tim then pointed to an entrance in the far corner, indicating a parking space that was just visible beyond.

'No sign of our friend Dima yet. Of course, other than him we have no idea who we are looking for.' Tim waved his arms in exasperation. 'Sadly, we have no photos of any of his operatives.'

He was now leaning through the open driver's window as Dom applied the handbrake, almost bent at right angles as his head was level with Dom. His breath smelt of freshly chewed mints. Dom wondered how much whisky Tim had drunk before he got the call late last night.

'Do we know where the Cabinet are?' Dom asked.

'Well, they have followed our advice and have all gone to the House of Commons Library. Rather than evacuate them, we decided to keep them in a secure location as we have no idea what form the attack will take. Only a minimal number of staff know their location. We have surrounded the building with a ring of steel. Don't forget that library is hidden within the Palace of Westminster and it withstood the blitz in the second world war!' Tim was clearly rising to the occasion.

Dom nodded. It made sense. An extremely efficient looking middle-aged woman was walking towards them. Ignoring Dom, she addressed Tim directly in hushed tones, having drawn him to one side, so that Dom could not hear the conversation. Tim was nodding thoughtfully and rubbing his chin with his palm earnestly as she spoke.

***

'Sorry about that,' Tim said, a few minutes later. 'That was Cheryl Massingham. Very sharp. A clever cookie. She is liaising with both us and Special Branch.' Dom noticed he was chewing on some fresh mints.

'I recognise the name. Isn't she in the Cabinet? Surely she should be with the rest of them?'

'Yes, but as the Minister for Security and Counter Terrorism, she has been released to head this whole thing up. One way of staying away from the threat, I suppose.'

Dom just about managed to keep up with Tim's stride as he walked across the quad towards the open door of the command room.

‘Follow me,’ Tim called behind, indicating to the stairs and pointing upwards. The old staircase wound up inside the two-hundred-year-old building and Tim scuttled up them and through doors at the top into a cavernous room. It was empty except for a large table in the middle, around which a group of young people were checking an array of computers and mobile phones. The table itself was strewn with coffee cups and crisp packets. Clearly these were more of Tim’s boffins.

‘Any news guys?’ Tim addressed the occupants en masse. There were a few murmurs, but nobody raised any significant progress. ‘Never mind.’ Tim clapped his hands enthusiastically. ‘Tea or coffee?’ He walked over to the kettle by a sink against the far wall. Dom was about to follow him, when he stopped dead in his tracks.

‘I forgot. I’ve got the phone! We may find something of use on that.’

‘What phone?’ Tim looked blank.

‘The one that I found on the assassin, Mike.’

Tim nodded as he continued to make the drinks. Dom handed over the mobile. Tim looked at it for a few seconds, deep in thought. He clearly didn’t expect me to manage to find any devices, Dom reflected.

‘This could be very useful,’ Tim mused.

‘Yes. You realise that they may not know Mike is dead, and therefore, more to the point, that we have his phone?'

Tim considered this. 'But, it was several hours ago since he last used it. Let's see shall we.' He logged on to the phone again and attempted to open the WhatsApp group Dom had looked at earlier.

'It's no use – I can't make head or tail of how to access the group chat and its message history.'

'Maybe I can help?'

They both looked around in the direction of the young woman who had spoken. Tim seemed slightly taken aback before he regained his composure and handed Dom his tea before he spoke.

'Dom, this is Mary. If anyone can get us into that network group under an assumed identity, Mary can. She's our top cyber expert. We've seconded her from GCHQ for the time being,' Tim explained. He handed the phone over. Dom thought Mary looked embarrassed by the verbose introduction she had been given.

Ten minutes later and she was back.

'I have managed to get in as J in WhatsApp.' Her tone was brisk and business-like. 'Well actually, it's not WhatsApp. It is an IP messaging system set up with its own encryption, activated by a WhatsApp shortcut icon. They've even mimicked the display – format, colour, all the settings basically. Completely unnoticeable to the untrained eye. A clever way to mask the messages under the cloak of WhatsApp, but actually easy to break into.'

'Great! Thanks, Mary.' Tim grabbed the phone off

of her. It's all gone over his head, Dom thought. 'Now we need to know what the last message was.' Tim continued. 'Hopefully we can get more information on the attack.' He sat deep in thought for at least a minute and Dom was about to suggest a plan of action, when Tim typed into the phone.

J: Repeat last instruction.

NJ: What, repeat request??

J: Repeat last instruction.

NJ: Frozen in because? [3,5]

Tim sighed and passed the phone to Dom. 'Great, another bloody crossword clue. Your shout, Dom!'

'Well, something to do with frozen and the "in" suggests it comes from the words following.' Dom scratched his head. 'Hang on, some of the letters forming "in because" can be rearranged to spell "ice cubes". That's the clue. The poison is in ice cubes. That must be the intended way of wiping out the Cabinet.'

CHAPTER TWENTY-SEVEN

The attack

Bunty tilted her head, in very slight acknowledgement, as she breezed past Jesse at the security gate, following the other waitress. It was just after eight thirty in the morning. The black uniform with the white cuffs and collar was identical to those shown in the caterer's publicity material. So far, none of the waiting staff, employed by an outside contractor, had realised she was not one of their employees. As she walked, she sensed Jesse following behind her. In her hand, Bunty held the large bowl containing the fruit salad, taken off the end of the preparation table in the kitchen a few seconds earlier. Once she had slowed a little, Jesse moved into the gap between Bunty and the other waitress walking ahead of her. Then with a nod of his head, he veered to the left, pushing open a door marked "Private – staff only" and entered the small locker room. Bunty watched as the waitress in front turned a corner and moved out of sight, and then followed Jesse through the open door.

'Here.' He spoke silently and motioned to Bunty to hand him the bowl. Emptying its contents into a black bin liner, he placed this in the waste bin, rearranging the rubbish above it so that it was hidden. Satisfied that it looked no different than before, he handed the bowl back and opened the locker.

'Keep perfectly still,' he hissed.

Bunty gulped as she watched Jesse use plastic tongs to carefully drop the ice blocks into the bowl, one by one. She counted thirty.

'Do we know the target yet? Did you manage to work out the cryptic clue?' she asked anxiously.

'Yes. It's the Cabinet who are the intended target,' Jesse replied. 'Now remember, make sure you start getting these into drinks as soon as you get inside the room.'

As she turned, the door opened and a young Asian woman entered. There was a brief pause as she stared at them both. Bunty could see the look of surprise in the woman's eyes as she looked inquiringly at Jesse.

'Just needed to clean up a small spillage,' Bunty explained, before adding, 'sorry!'

'You shouldn't be in here. Make sure this doesn't happen again, Jesse.' She glared at Bunty.

He nodded. 'Sorry, Shaz. I was just helping this lady clean up the mess.'

As they were talking, Bunty made her exit,

unnoticed. Heading down the corridor, she moved up the flight of stairs and followed the route she had been given by Jesse. However, this time, if anyone had been watching, they would have seen she moved slightly more slowly, taking care and making sure she carried her load precisely. The corridor was silent, although she could hear talk coming from the direction she was heading. The light was weak, just strong enough for her to navigate her way along the thick braid carpet without any mishaps.

In just over a minute, she was entering the large room where the Cabinet were deep in discussion. All the sound came from the direction of the long table at the far corner, around which members of the Cabinet were seated, while all the other inhabitants moved noiselessly in the background, not wishing to draw any attention. Perfect, Bunty thought to herself. This was likely to be even easier than she had expected. She headed over to the far counter to where a man who appeared to be in charge of hospitality was beckoning her. He looked somewhat crestfallen when she placed the bowl of fresh ice down, as if he had been dealt a poor hand of cards. Bunty smiled, standing back. She smoothed down the apron on the front of her uniform – the perfect example of the conscientious waitress. Mindful of the instructions from Jesse, she picked up the first of a row of glasses that had been filled with orange juice and held the thin stem as she moved to pick up the ice with the tongs that were also in the bowl.

It all happened so quickly, it took Dom by surprise, even though he had been fully briefed. One minute, everything in the room was normal, then the maître d' leant over and forcibly took the glass out of Bunty's hand. Taken unawares, she let it slip out of her grasp, until she realised too late, by which time the plain-clothes security officer had handcuffed her other hand. Several members of the Cabinet turned around at the ensuing commotion, aware that the attack they had been warned against may be about to take place.

As she was led away, Tim moved over to Dom and spoke quietly in his ear. 'We now need to locate the other agents. She can't have been working alone. Somebody else must have brought the stuff in and helped her transfer it.'

Dom nodded. It made sense. It had already struck him that it was highly unlikely the woman was working on her own. He saw that Cheryl Massingham had arrived in the room. Tim was speaking quietly into her left ear, presumably giving her an update. Out of the corner of his eye, Dom noticed a staff member – a tall, good-looking man, presumably an aide to one of the ministers – making a hasty retreat as inconspicuously as possible via the main door.

'Hey, chase him!' Dom surprised himself with the authority he used. The security guard stared at Dom and looked to Tim for confirmation. Tim nodded and the guard shot off in hot pursuit.

A few minutes later, the man was dragged back into the room by the security guard and marched over in the direction of Cheryl Massingham and Tim.

'Paul?' Cheryl stared at the young man, confusion clear on her face.

'Check his pockets. Any sign of a phone?'

The guard held up a small burner phone. Tim nodded and further security staff appeared and led the man away in handcuffs.

Tim turned to Cheryl. 'Did you know him?'

'I can't believe it. Paul – he's my personal advisor. He was my right-hand man. My confidant.' Shocked, Cheryl moved to sit on a nearby chair.

'I hate to break it to you, but it seems you were central to their plans.' Tim outlined the planned attack as Cheryl stared in disbelief. 'With all the Cabinet poisoned, you would have been in a position to take control by default as Prime Minister.'

'But why?' Cheryl stared at him.

'Well, it seems Paul had earmarked you as a sympathiser to an enemy state.'

'Never. Not of this. Not like this!' Cheryl shook her head vehemently.

'Well perhaps he felt he could convince you, influence you.' Tim nodded wryly. 'He was obviously confident he could get you to do his bidding.'

Cheryl stared at the floor. She suddenly felt sick. Sick, old and foolish.

***

The cold morning air hit Bunty's face as she was marched in handcuffs towards the waiting police van. Out of the corner of her eye, she caught the woman she had reported to an hour earlier glaring over, deep in conversation with a policeman, cigarette dangling from between her fingers.

'Bloody crafty cow. Yes, I did check her name. She came up as being registered as one of our temps. The ID she gave me matched the name. She already had a company ID badge anyway.'

The woman shrugged her shoulders, making it clear that she was not to blame for Bunty's presence. She took a further defiant drag on the cigarette.

Bunty turned away. They had reached the van and she was bundled unceremoniously into the black void, the door slammed and locked behind her. Nobody else was in the van. No sign of Jesse. Presumably he had avoided detection. Bunty wondered if the supervisor who saw them together had reported it yet to the police and security staff. She imagined the woman would realise it was too much of a coincidence. She expected Jesse to be thrown in beside her at any minute. Instead, when the door opened, it was by a police armed response unit officer, in full gear, holding an automatic rifle. Avoiding Bunty's stare, she sat opposite, pointing the gun directly at her, as the van started to move. She could see nothing as the van drove out of the grounds of the Palace of Westminster. The small black glass windows were in a row down either side of the van, several feet above her head. Instead, the light came from one neon bulkhead, positioned in the centre of the ceiling behind what looked like toughened, or even bulletproof, glass. This gave the officer enough visibility to clearly see the prisoner sitting two feet away from her.

Bunty thought of Bryan, standing patiently in front of the latest display of cheese, explaining the virtues of each as his watchful eye checked on any petty thefts that never occurred. Bryan, who chatted to the locals as they dropped off their post. She could hear him now, explaining how Bunty would be returning armed with the latest information to make the post office run more efficiently. Her eyes began to water. How could she explain all this to him? His realisation that their life had been a lie would be crushing. Could she ever even face him again? Bunty knew the answer: memories would heal the wounds over time. With that thought in her mind, she made her decision.

Soon, the van slowed to a halt. The door opened and the officer gestured for Bunty to dismount. Bunty tried to stand, but with her hands cuffed it was clear that she could not get the leverage she needed from her short, unathletic legs. As she sat down again, the officer turned to call that some assistance was needed, whilst keeping the gun fixed on her. In that split second, when their gaze was elsewhere, Bunty moved her hand to her sleeve and then to her face. The small 500 mg capsule was in her mouth as she bit hard on its thin shell. As the contents emptied into her system, she began to lose consciousness. Within a minute, she was dead.

CHAPTER TWENTY-EIGHT

Escape

Leaning on the railing on the top deck, Jesse drew deeply on his cigarette. It was a cold afternoon and the decking was deserted as the sea mist closed in. He had boarded the ferry from Felixstowe as a foot passenger, having abandoned the motorbike down one of the many side streets that led down to the docks. He cast his mind back to the previous three hours.

He had seen both the other agents led away. Firstly, the tall communist, who he had never really warmed to or trusted. It was true that the man was good-looking, but he clearly knew this and played on it. Jesse knew vanity was a weakness and he wondered whether this had contributed to the failure of the attack. He was never sure about the integrity of those who did not do it for money. In his experience, those motivated by a cause were more likely to change their mind than if they were driven by pure greed. Money always talked in Jesse's opinion. Bunty was different, of course. She was as fervent as Dima and the cause was her life. But generally, Jesse had come to believe that money was the best motivator. Many people would do almost anything for money. In fact, they just wanted to know that they had not thrown the final stone, or the last blow. No, he was never convinced by the guy. But, when he was led away protesting his innocence, Jesse had wondered if he might convince the authorities it was a case of mistaken identity. However, less than a minute later, Bunty was marched out in handcuffs in full view of the security gate where he was seated. That was when he knew the game was up and he had to make his escape. It would not take long for the police to hear from his supervisor that he had been seen with Bunty in the staff room. The authorities would already be searching for a contact with inside knowledge of the buildings and it wouldn't take long to work it out.

Jesse wandered casually off towards the toilets. Less than twenty yards away was his motorcycle. He broke into a run and started the bike. With no leathers or helmet, he had no choice but to drive off in his full security gear. As he had expected, the barrier was down as he approached the gate. At the last minute, he accelerated, turning away as the wood and metal barrier fractured, splintering everywhere. Ahead was the main external gate. A much tougher proposition – it had a bulletproof metal barrier to stop terrorist attacks. Instead, he used his knowledge of the grounds and headed for a small pedestrian gate with a wooden barrier and security post. He crossed the freshly mown lawn in front of it at full throttle, bullets raining down behind him as he attempted his escape. From a nearby building, he could hear a siren and a voice over the tannoy informing all unarmed staff and visitors to evacuate. Startled pedestrians fled as he joined the concrete walkway that led to the gate.

It was almost prophetic that Ed was on duty at that post at that time. His usual swagger was gone as he saw Jesse bear down on him, replaced by a look of abject horror. He just managed to jump aside as the bike moved past, almost unhindered by its last obstacle.

Of course, there had been a police pursuit, an assortment of cars and motorbikes, which he soon evaded. Then the helicopters hovered above, shining their lights. But he had managed to escape them all. There had been a reason why he had taken a different route back after each shift and the knowledge had paid off. On the edge of Epping Forest, he found a large area to dismount, remove the security gear and change the number plates – a relatively easy task of removing an outer plastic film to reveal a new number.

His last action before reaching the ferry was to alert Dima of the plan's failure. Taking out the burner, he sent the agreed message.

Rob Ken! [anag]

***

'Blast!' Tim Coutts removed the phone from his right ear and turned to face Dom. 'Bad news. They have just been to apprehend Dima and there is no sign of him at the flat. Just a very angry ex-girlfriend. Apparently, he did a runner while she was out at the shops. Classy, I must say. He took her car as well. Sadly, Marcus missed spotting him leaving. They're trying to trace the car as we speak, so I'm waiting for an update.'

At that moment, the phone rang again. Tim listened intently for nearly a minute.

'They've found her car, abandoned near Kew station, parked down a side road. The good news is we have issued an all-ports alert, so hopefully he shouldn't get far.'

'Surely he won't travel under his own passport?' said Dom.

'No, he will have a completely new identity, I'm sure. We just have to hope he hasn't changed his appearance too much. His height at least should be unchanged.'

'It's a real pity we didn't catch him before he left. After all, we even knew where he was staying,' Dom reflected.

'Yes,' Tim reflected. 'Not Marcus's finest hour, I must say.'

CHAPTER TWENTY-EIGHT

Exit

Dima glanced at the faded blue motorway sign as he moved the car into fifth gear and overtook the Belgian juggernaut, which was struggling to climb the steep incline, smoke billowing from its exhaust. He caught the white writing before it disappeared from view: Dover, twenty-three miles. Drawing level with the truck's cab, he saw the overweight driver playing with his mobile phone and drinking from a coffee cup, one eye occasionally on the road. Nothing about the overtaking vehicle made the lorry driver give it any more than the minimal attention. Dima smiled to himself as he considered the modest Japanese saloon Jesse had purchased for him from a less reputable motor trader, based in an anonymous South London backstreet. Fitted with false plates, it was one of several million of the model sold in the UK during a period of ten years. The bland matt-black finish was perfect to blend into the steady stream of motorists heading to the channel ports. Of course, he would rather be in a flash convertible, but that would have to wait until after he had completed his exit. Checking the rear mirror, he was pleased to see there was still no sign of anyone following him.

Dima felt a slight twinge of regret about the way he had left Shona, but there was no time for sentiment. He would never be returning, never see her again. That much was certain. A swift return to the Motherland was essential before he was associated with the failed attack. If the British worked out he had been pulling the strings, he would be hauled in. They would do everything they could to tempt him to pass over all he knew – operations, names, locations. If his own side worked out he had failed, it would be worse, much worse. Most likely he would be removed quietly, so no questions could be asked. The best he could hope for would be endless hours of claustrophobic questioning in a small, soulless room, similar to the one he had shared with Tanya during the brief first assignation. Dima shuddered when he thought of it. He would need to get back to the country somehow and lie low. There were people and places he knew where he would be safe from the authorities for the time being.

***

Dima had seized his chance to leave the flat at short

notice about two hours earlier. He had been trying to monitor the attack via contact with his agents using their burner mobiles. It soon became obvious where it was heading. Coming into the lounge from the kitchen, Shona was beginning to look frustrated. After all, she had expected to get more attention than the phone. Dima looked up, excuse at the ready.

'I need to check my shares. Russian oil and gas.' He could hear himself saying it now, sounding like the voice of a legitimate trader. 'You never know, I may have become a billionaire!' he added, rather optimistically.

She nodded, accepting his excuse. 'I'll just nip to the supermarket. We are low on fruit and milk.' Maybe she knew he was about to leave, as he had done before, without saying goodbye. Maybe she had hardened herself to it.

After a brief peck on the cheek, she closed the flat door and he soon heard her descend the stairs a few seconds later. It was an inglorious departure and he knew she would feel cheated when she returned later to the empty flat to find him gone. But perhaps she expected it. Maybe that was why she had chosen to leave, giving him the opportunity to disappear whilst she was absent. No sign, bags packed and taken. Cheated and used. He tried not to think about it. Instead, he wondered if any of the agents had escaped. Once he had realised Mike had been killed, he knew the attack was on the back foot. It had been a calculated gamble to keep all his key agents abreast of the plans – something he now deeply regretted, but at the time it had made the operation easier to manage and faster to execute. Sadly, it had also been its downfall. The final message from Jesse at least alerted him to the failure and gave him a fighting chance to make an exit. He had managed to send a final message of his own, but from his controller there had been nothing.

***

However, it was all about self-preservation now. Dima ran his hand over the false beard as it clung begrudgingly to his face. The itching was something he would have to live with until he had at least cleared all countries en route that were under the watchful eye of Interpol. He knew his photograph would have been widely circulated. The shaved head had been a very simple idea, yet he felt it was a masterstroke. All that he had needed was a motorway toilet stop and a battery driven shaver. Afterwards, still inside the cubicle, he had massaged a small amount of fake tan into his exposed scalp and was pleased to note the face that stared back at him in the mirror could have been mistaken for a Romanian farm worker. If he was stopped before he left the UK, his cover story was a seasonal fruit picker returning to the Caucasus. The lowly car and lack of luggage bore testament to this. Once he reached Romania, he would head north into Russia. Any checkpoints then would be unlikely to have the information supplied by the UK. He would breeze through with his native Russian and a suitable banknote donation to that night's card game at the checkpoint. Once he had crossed the frontier, he would be able to locate friends he could stay with for a month or so, whilst a new identity was created. That would be the easiest part.

But for now, he must concentrate on the identity he had just been given. Looking down, Dima smiled as he saw the faded passport on the passenger seat beside him. A wonderful piece of work from an excellent forger – a friend he had used in the past, based at the back of a second-hand jewellers in Soho. It was a good touch to have hair in the photograph; they would need to compare this to his shaved head, hopefully reducing time they would spend looking for anything else. It was even worth wearing the fake beard to get such a good likeness. The passport was in the name of a low-profile Russian businessman, a regular traveller, living in blissful ignorance in a quiet cul de sac in Princes Risborough, his wife and daughters likely to be by his side as they ate their meal this evening and then watched a film on their favourite streaming service.

As the harbour came into sight, Dima slowed down to the speed limit of thirty miles per hour and took his place in the single line of vehicles snaking to enter the Eastern docks area. The day on the channel coast was unseasonably warm and the sun was beating down onto the concrete arm, which stretched like a tentacle away from the shoreline and into the sea. Soon, he was through passport control, with a weary nod from a tired-looking Border Force official, probably nearing the end of a ten-hour shift, and was parking up in the large car park in front of the berth, as the cross-channel ferry finished disembarking.

There had been none of the tension he felt when he had entered the country. After all, he had nothing concealed, nothing to hide this time as he had strolled confidently through the deserted customs area. In front of him, the large screen displayed the sailing times, flashing in neon LEDs on a large outdoor billboard. He saw he had just over half an hour before the Calais ferry would start loading.

Dima allowed his mind to drift to possible plans once he had finally managed to secure his escape. A friend who lived at a quiet Black Sea resort owed him a favour from years back. He would stay there for a few months until the heat had died down. Lying on a sunbed with a cold beer in his hand, keeping his head down, whilst he swam amongst the holidaymakers. He could picture it now, everybody either reading or drinking, before a short swim to cool off. Not such a bad life. There were certainly worse ways to pass the time. And he was almost there. He smiled to himself. He would survive and return again, stronger. He always did.

As he opened the driver's door, he felt the heat rise off the large expanse of faded black tarmac. Was this really the UK? It felt more like a port on the Mediterranean, but without the constant beat of the cicadas. The tannoy announcing that another ferry for Ostend was about to load was followed by the sound of engines coming to life, the air filling with exhaust fumes. He could taste the petroleum in his already dry mouth. A sign above the small, shabby, grey restaurant block showed it was also the location of the toilets. His throat was parched; his tonsils felt sore and swallowing was becoming painful. Dima could not remember when he had last had a drink.

Heading towards the open doors, he saw a young woman standing at the side of the entrance in a company uniform, smiling as she handed over ice cold bottles of water to the incoming customers. It was a nice touch. Along with the other travellers, he gratefully took one. A brunette, she looked somehow familiar. He was so thirsty now he gratefully gulped the bottle down in one go.

'There is no ice in that.' The Eastern European accent cut through the crisp air. As he turned, he saw the long legs walk away in the distance, until his vision began to blur. By then, he was already falling, fighting for consciousness, as the Novichok took hold.

Concerned families were forced to stop, as he lay convulsing, blocking the entrance to the building. An ambulance was called.

***

A hundred yards away, the tall woman was opening a large black landfill wheelie bin, parked with several others behind the back wall of the complex. She disposed of a curly brown wig, revealing her blonde hair. Looking around to check she had not been followed, she took out her phone and spoke softly into it in Russian.

'I can report that the necklace has been destroyed. I repeat, the necklace has been destroyed!'

Without waiting for a reply, she threw the phone in after the wig and closed the large swing lid, walking quickly over to the shiny red two-seater sports car waiting nearby. As she sat down in the passenger seat, the driver, an attractive athletic man, leant over and pecked her lightly on the cheek, before engaging first gear and driving over to join the queue of vehicles now embarking on the ferry.

CHAPTER TWENTY-NINE

One week later

That Marcus had returned was evident as soon as Dom arrived. No longer was he greeted by the overpowering smell of dog when Tim opened the door; instead, he detected the subtle waft from a sandalwood diffuser, and as he entered, the house appeared to have experienced what could be best described as a deep clean. Classical music, possibly Wagner, failed to drown out the sound of a vacuum cleaner labouring away on the floor above. Even Tim's office had not escaped untouched. The cut glass tumblers were already positioned neatly on small mats to avoid staining the wooden desk, which gleamed when the sun flowed in through the window, the curtains smartly pulled back.

As Tim gestured for him to sit down, Dom noticed that he was wearing a crisply ironed cotton shirt with gold cufflinks; evidently the makeover had extended beyond the house. In fact, on closer inspection, Dom was sure that Tim had had his eyebrows trimmed slightly. They certainly appeared more well-kept than usual. And hadn't he spotted a flash of white from where Tim's few remaining teeth had once resided? Less crusty clerical academic and more suave fund manager, Dom thought to himself. There was an open copy of *The Telegraph* on the table in front of him.

'So, congratulations all round!' Tim continued. 'And your part in the stopping of the attack has not gone unnoticed, I can tell you,' he continued brightly. Dom nodded his thanks. Then his eyes strayed to a new edition to the wall behind Tim. Amongst the framed degrees and diplomas and smiling family group photos, celebrating some occasion or other, he saw the large framed certificate, proudly taking centre stage, proclaiming Tim the recipient of an award for services to counter terrorism. Tim followed his eyes and then lowered his head and coughed, rather apologetically.

'Ah, yes. Well, they insisted. Of course, it is really a reflection on the team rather than just one person. Anyway, as I said, you yourself have been mentioned in dispatches. Solving the cryptic clues was invaluable, Dom. Absolutely crucial to getting a successful outcome. Head office are very keen for you to take on more roles in future. We will clear it with your employer, of course,' Tim continued, unabashed.

Dom thought to himself. Maybe he should do this more often. Yes, there was the danger, but that was offset by the satisfaction of a good result. He had been warned when he started that this was not real life. Death was real enough though. His mind raced back to the all too familiar pile of low-quality work, waiting to be marked. Hardly inspiring. True, he felt bad that Dima's body had been found in the docks, but he had been assured that it had not been the work of our side.

'Sad about Dima though,' Dom reflected.

'Good riddance, I say. A bloody pain in the arse from start to finish,' Tim spluttered. 'Good riddance to bad rubbish. Now he's gone, they will be sorting a replacement of course. But it gives us a little breathing space, nevertheless. The smart money is on Tanya Kornikova. A little more of a challenge to us than Dima, she certainly had the making of him. The CCTV indicates she dealt the fatal blow, using a drink with Novichok in it. Would you believe it? So it was used on our shores, after all, but to silence one of their own!'

Plainly, Tim relished Dima's demise and the ironic manner of it. Dom, however, felt at least some remorse. Dima had been a friend. A good friend and an important part of his life. He would just have to toughen up, he reflected.

The doorbell rang and Tim jumped up, smiling over to Dom. Clearly, he had been waiting for this next part of the theatre he was playing out. As Tim left the room, Dom wondered what the next little charade would be, presumably something involving Marcus, or another of Tim's cronies.

‘Won’t be a second!’ He even winked, something Dom found distinctly off-putting. A minute later, he returned, followed by a familiar face.

‘Penny!’ Dom jumped out of his seat and embraced her. ‘What are you doing here?’

As she opened her mouth to answer, Tim interjected. ‘Penny is joining our ranks, Dom.’

‘Really!’ Dom showed genuine surprise. He had been impressed by Penny’s sensible and no-nonsense attitude, but would she really want all the hassle that came with this role?

‘Well, yes. I quite enjoyed the research and the tracking down.’ Penny spoke for the first time.

‘Oh yes,’ Tim interjected. ‘Penny already has a new assignment. Which, of course, she will be working on with you, Dom,’ he added quickly, attempting to avoid any possible ruffling of feathers.

‘Really?’ said Dom, conscious he was repeating himself. It was such a shock.

‘Yes. An ex-Fleet Street journalist, who now resides in a sleepy village in Southern Spain, has come to our notice. It seems he has been fraternising with a group who wish to overthrow a stable North African republic. We will be working jointly with their security forces. Penny will be in the ideal position to interview him on the premise of a book she is researching for a client.’

‘And me?’ Dom inquired. ‘Let me guess. Fluent French speaker?’

‘That’s it,’ said Tim. ‘Now, let me show the exact location on the map I have here on the desk.’ He started to lean over the desk and then stopped. ‘We need to celebrate! I’ll just get the champagne I have on ice.’

After Tim had departed, Dom turned to see Penny staring intently at the wall behind the desk. He was about to make a somewhat facetious comment along the lines that Tim hardly deserved the award, when he realised she was looking at an entirely different spot. Following her eyes, he saw the small colour photo in the middle in a silver frame above the fireplace. Seeing he was also looking at the photo, Penny pointed at the man standing at the far right of the group. As Dom looked more closely, he saw the face he had last seen on the lifeless body sprawled on the sand at Readymoney Cove. There were three other men in the photo, all of a similar age. Immediately, Dom felt a nausea rising within his stomach as he saw another familiar face. At the same time, Tim was returning with the champagne and three flutes.

‘Ah, yes. Marcus and his buddies. They called themselves the four musketeers.’

‘And where is Marcus now, Tim?’ Dom asked quietly.

‘Well upstairs cleaning, of course. You can hear the vacuum. Not that I see that is any of your business.’ Tim was beginning to sound irritated.

‘I think you had better check, Tim?’ It was Penny

speaking now, taking the lead. Tim stared at her. Then, after nearly a minute, it appeared to dawn on him. Seconds later, he was bounding up the stairs, three at a time with those long legs, shouting at the top of his voice.

'Marcus! Come down here, can you?'

Dom and Penny waited downstairs, whilst the noise of doors slamming and the vacuum being switched off came from above. About ten minutes later, a crestfallen Tim returned.

'Nothing. The little shit has gone. Taken all his possessions. He must have made off once you had arrived. Clever trick leaving the hoover on though. Found it wedged on its back in a cupboard!' He looked at them both for a moment. 'I always wondered how they managed to track down Dima before he left the country. Marcus must have tipped off Tanya Kornikova. All the time he was watching Dima for us, he was in the perfect position to pass the information on to them as well.'

'A double agent!' Dom whistled.

'Well, hardly.' Tim cleared his throat. 'He was my clerical assistant, not a spy exactly, Dom. And in some ways, that makes the betrayal even worse,' he said, shaking his head sadly.

CHAPTER THIRTY

The final clue

As they were leaving later, Dom was taken aback when Penny suggested they go for a quick coffee. There was, she informed him, a small coffee kiosk with an outdoor seating area in the small park at the top of Tim's road.

'What's so important?' Dom asked, when they were finally seated.

He stared at Penny's herbal tea, wishing he had made a healthier choice than the large cappuccino.

'Don't you think it's strange that Marcus managed to work for Tim for so long without being exposed?' she replied, in between sips.

'Well…' Dom considered it slowly. 'Not really. He must have been careful to stay well under the radar. Especially if he intended to use his position to help the Necklace spy ring with their attack.'

'I'm not so sure.'

'Well, Tim would have spotted it, surely?'

'Unless he knew all along?'

'Never, no way!' Dom was shaking his head now. 'Tim can't have known. He recruited me, remember? Look how surprised he was to see Marcus had gone.'

'We only have his word for that. Did we actually go upstairs and check where Marcus was?'

Dom considered this. Penny had a point. They hadn't checked.

'Did you ask yourself why he recruited you? Or me, for that matter?' Penny continued. 'Where was the back-up you were expecting at Readymoney Cove, for example?'

It was true, Dom reflected. There was never any sign of the back-up he had been promised.

'But he sent me there to watch you,' he said, still shaking his head.

'Maybe, or maybe he sent you to your death, with me, at the hands of his assassin.'

'Well, hang on. His assassin? Surely, he could have blown our operation at any time? After all, he was overseeing the whole thing,' Dom persisted.

'Maybe he did. Don't forget, he wants to stay in this role for as long as he can. What happened exactly with the failed attempt to stop the handover of the Novichok?' she asked.

'I had to leave to take a call from Tim. That village hall was in the middle of nowhere and the reception was terrible.'

'Exactly!'

‘But he couldn’t have known. He wasn’t there. How could he have got the timing right? His bods were monitoring it all from a removal van in the next village...’ His voice trailed off. ‘Anyway, he needed me. To solve the cryptic crossword clues. He couldn’t do that.’

‘Did you see his copy of today’s *Telegraph*?’

He didn’t see how this was relevant.

‘Yes, on his desk. Why?’

‘I flicked to the crossword. The cryptic crossword, not the general knowledge one. It was completed, and signed and dated.’

‘It could have been Marcus?’ Dom felt himself clutching at straws.

‘It was Tim’s signature. I saw it on a claim form on his desk.’

‘I have to say, he did sound surprised to hear from me when I called him before we left Cornwall,’ Dom reflected.

‘And how did he respond when you gave him the phone you took off Mike?’ Penny spoke once more. ‘After all, that provided enough information to identify the location and target of the attack.’

‘Well. To be fair, he didn’t seem to see the importance of the phone. It was lucky that Mary was there. She overheard me reminding Tim and took it away. Her contacts managed to get logged into the WhatsApp messages when Tim couldn’t...’ Dom’s voice trailed off as he realised what he had just said. Oh no. How had he been fooled? It seemed so obvious now.

The conversation was broken by the loud arrival of a group of people at the table next to them. Out of the corner of his eye, Dom saw several of the adults seated in the group wore casual shirts with neckerchiefs held in toggles – scout leaders. Inside the depths of his brain, a small cog turned. He looked at Penny.

'What was that clue again, the one we still need to solve?'

Penny flicked through her phone, reading out loud, '***One less this time for tea with scout [3,6].***'

Dom racked his brain. Still, he could see no solution and was in the process of handing the mobile back when he saw something in the clue.

'Hang on. Tea could stand for just the letter "T". If you add that to the word scout, to make "tea with scout" then you have an anagram of Coutts. Surely, that can't be a coincidence?'

'Yes, and "one less this time" means take away the last letter of "time", giving you "Tim",' Penny continued.

'But why would Dima send this to you by email?' Dom was shaking his head. 'It just doesn't make sense.'

'It must have been his insurance. If he got caught, he was going to take Tim down with him. He was banking on us not solving this and passing it to Tim. We know

Tim can solve them and he would realise he had to get Dima out or he would talk and take him down with him.'

'So this was Dima's insurance policy?'

'Yes. Dima sent this as a signal. Basically a warning to Tim. After all, if anyone could ensure Dima's safe passage, it would be Tim. What he didn't know, of course, was that Tim had moved on. He had a new ally.

'Who?'

'Tanya Kornikova. Don't forget, Tim knew where Dima was. It was easy enough to trace him covertly and pass the location to her without letting the rest of us know.'

Dom's head was swimming. What a fool he'd been! In the background, he could hear Penny relaying Tim Coutts's address to DCI Evans.

CHAPTER THIRTY-ONE

Epilogue

The small dog stood rigidly by his master's side, waiting for a command, as the elderly man leaned forward and placed the flowers beside the plaque. The stone was fresh, with clean gold lettering, unlike those surrounding it, which were faded and tinged with green algae. Bryan had ensured there was enough space below for the two lines that would bear his own brief details. They had agreed on that long ago. He kissed his palm and then leant forward and gently placed his open hand against the cold stone. He looked down at the dog.

'Just you and me now, lad.'

Bryan shook his head as he walked away, hands clasped tightly behind his back. What had she been thinking of? The details were sketchy, but he knew that type of poison in capsule form suggested she was an integral part of the attack. As the dog looked up at him with big innocent eyes, he held back the tears as he gently patted its head. Then he turned abruptly and made his way out of the churchyard and across the lane towards the shop, now permanently closed with a "For sale" sign attached to the front wall. He opened the back door and disappeared inside, the faithful terrier trotting in behind him.

Acknowledgements

A big thank you to Kirsty at Cranthorpe Millner for taking a chance on me as a debut novelist and to Lydia and Vicky for their support with the editing of the book and Shannon and Donna for overseeing its marketing.

Finally, thanks to Sarah for her support and for being with me every step of the way on this journey.

CPSIA information can be obtained
at www.ICGtesting.com
Printed in the USA
BVHW030454200123
656704BV00003B/74

9 781803 780924